The Poet in Exile

The Poet in Exile

THUNDER'S MOUTH PRESS
NEW YORK

THE POET IN EXILE
© 2001 by Ray Manzarek

Published by
Thunder's Mouth Press
An Imprint of Avalon Publishing Group Incorporated
161 William St., 16th Floor
New York, NY 10038

Library of Congress Cataloging-in-Publication Data is available for this title.

ISBN 1-56025-359-2

9 8 7 6 5 4 3 2 1

Designed by Michael Walters

Printed in the United States of America
Distributed by Publishers Group West

His eyes had gotten kinder. Kindess came finally to the better ones. There was less self-interest. Less fear. Less competitive gamesmanship.

Charles Bukowski: "Hollywood"

The Poet in Exile

1

I received the first letter from the Poet a little over six months ago. I knew it was from him, but that was impossible. He was dead. He was buried in Paris in the 1970s. In one of those charming, *Jules and Jim*, tree-lined, flower-bedecked, mausoleum-encrusted cemeteries so favored by artists, poets, composers, stray cats, and romantically obsessed young girls. He was buried in a simple morning ceremony attended by only five people: his mistress, two French friends, his manager and his secretary. The manager reported a sealed coffin. He never saw the body. The secretary merely attended the funeral and then drifted on to other lives. The mistress retreated into heroin and died of an overdose three years after the Poet's death. Only the two French friends knew the truth and they weren't talking. Not to the press, not to me, not to anyone.

Could the rumors of one hundred and fifty pounds of sand in a sealed coffin be true? A coffin said to be sealed "for the sake of propriety." And what of the Algerian doctor? His signature on the death certificate is said to have been purchased for $5,000 American, a not insubstantial sum in 1970s money. Could it be true? The death certificate says his heart stopped, nothing more. No cause of death, no suspicion of foul play, no death by misadventure, no trauma, no autopsy, nothing. His heart simply stopped. However, given his excessive life style—the drinking, the drugs, the women—and the toll it took on his physical condition, it did seem as if the final payment had come due.

Or was it, in fact, a hoax? Was it all an elaborate ruse to free the Poet from his worldly entanglements, including his now increasingly heroin-intoxicated mistress, and send him off to ports unknown where he could pursue his craft unencumbered? Free of his rock-and-roll lifestyle, the pressures of fame and its demands on his time and his psyche. Free of his sycophants and his "drinking buddies"—the La Brea Mafia—who laughed too long and too loudly at his jokes. Free of the shrill demands of journalists who hounded him in search of the *bon mot*, or a revelation of the psychological imperative that made the Poet write.

"What was he really like?" they asked me after his death. I felt like Marlene Dietrich at the end of *Touch of Evil*. "He was some kind of man. What does it matter what you say about people?" Did they expect me to reveal the secrets of our relationship? The hidden, private moments that belonged only to us? Or did they expect me to sum up a Dionysian life in a paragraph? The Poet's needs and visions, the cosmic flights and psychic journeys, the explorations of consciousness that drove him relentlessly belonged to him. If he had chosen to share them with me, they belonged to us. And only us. His dark and peculiar genius was in the music, and the rest was not for public consumption.

Besides, he was far too complex for a tidy summing-up. He was an artist of the first order and the most passionate person I have ever known. Categories could not contain him.

And we were going to change the world. Until the seduction of fame conquered the best of us. Until the seduction of easy money, easy drugs and too-easy women destroyed the best minds of the post-beatnik generation. The Poet, aware of his descent, had gone to Paris to try to save himself and to flee the enervation of the seduction. He was attempting to recapture the muse, to write again. To write his words, his poems, his stories. But he died—tragically, suddenly, and very mysteriously. He died too early and too young, his great work left unrealized, his promise unfulfilled. A tragic cloud passed over me with his death, and it was, for a long time, impossible to accept the fact that I had lost my friend forever. It took many years to finally let him go.

And then the letter came. Like so many other fan letters requesting an autograph or a picture of the band. Letters from around the world. But this one caught my eye. It bore a very colorful stamp. The fruit of the coco-de-mer, shaped like the hips of a woman, set against an azure sea and a golden beach. A picture of paradise and the intoxicating sensuality of the tropics. I immediately thought of the Poet's lines: "Tropic passage, tropic bounty. How have we come so far? To this lush equator." I opened the letter to see what this fan would have to say . . . and was jolted. The words were written in a familiar scrawl.

> *Roy:*
>
> *The eternity of diamond consciousness*
> *makes this Herculean task seem almost worth*
> *the price of admission.*
>
> *J.*

There was nothing more. This Zen haiku-like three liner could not possibly be from the Poet. And yet it was his hand and his style. But how could he be alive? And if he was, what did this missive mean? Was it a statement of his condition? Did he need my help? And was it even him?

But this cryptic note containing both sides of the coin was a message that flooded me with images of loss and a destiny only partially fulfilled. And as I read the words over and over I felt an exhilaration rise in me, leaving me breathless and on the verge of tears. My God, he's alive! It didn't end in Paris, there's actually more to come!

But then reality intruded. What if it's a sham, I thought. What if it's an evil little ruse from the negatively charged psyche of someone like that witchy woman who purports to be "channeling" the Poet. She sends nasty little notes to me and the other two— the guitar player and the drummer—admonishing us for carrying on without the Poet, or for keeping his name alive, or for keeping our music alive, or, hell, for *being* alive. The notes are always evil and dark, filled with the negative truth of the paranoid. Probably fueled by crystal meth and its accompanying mind-set, an insanity that generates its own reality, the upside-down, inside-out reality that appears to them to be the real truth behind everything.

I quickly picked up the envelope, afraid of what the postmark would reveal. If it was stamped Los Angeles it was from the succubus and I would toss the damned thing from my sight. Instead, it was even more magical than I could have hoped for. Inked onto that envelope, next to that lovely stamp of the coco-de-mer, was a circle that said "The Seychelle Islands," the date and the time of posting. The Seychelles! That little group of islands lost in the Indian Ocean, somewhere between the subcontinent of India and the east coast of Africa. It was real.

And then I remembered a conversation we had had not two weeks before he left for Paris. He asked me if I had ever heard of the Seychelles.

"The sea shells?" I said.

"No," he said. "Seychelles . . . somewhere in the middle of the Indian Ocean. A little group of islands. Way off the beaten track."

I had to admit I hadn't heard of them.

"The coconut tree bears fruit shaped like a woman's hips," he said. "Very lush, very sexual. I've got a travel brochure. Here, take a look."

He handed me a four-page color pamphlet. The islands looked gorgeous, and virtually inaccessible, sitting there in the upper middle of the Indian Ocean. "Beautiful," I said as I handed it back to him.

"Yeah," he said. "A man could really disappear in a place like that."

I nodded, and never gave it another thought. Until now. And then it all fell into place. The bastard had done it. Lighted out for the territory, somewhere northeast of Madagascar and due east of Mombassa on the African coast. He had probably been there all these years, living a Somerset Maugham life in the tropics, relaxed, rested, and writing. Or maybe he just used the Seychelles as home base and spent his time traveling through the Orient. Or maybe he was on a Joseph Conrad–like search. A search for meaning.

But how was he living? On *what* was he living? All his royalties went to his family. They had at first gone to his mistress, but when she succumbed to the dragon, the money went to his next of kin. Were they secretly funneling money to the Seychelles? I couldn't picture it. He had broken with his family, never making contact with them, to the best of my knowledge, after we graduated together from the university.

And what about his identity? Did he have a forged passport? He couldn't be using his own name. He was too well known. But had they heard of him in the remote Seychelles?

There were so many questions. I was overflowing with them. They raced around in my brainpan, chasing each other and howling and squealing for attention. But they all took second position to the one main question: Was something wrong? And if so, what was I to do? Why didn't he say more? Why didn't he include an address? How could I help him if I didn't know where he was? I looked at the envelope again, and I *did* know where he was. He was in the Seychelles.

The next few days were lived in a fog. I could only think about him and what to do to help him if this turned out to be real. And then another letter came, from the Seychelles.

> *Roy:*
> *Perfumed hair. Painted lips.*
> *I enfolded her in my arms*
> *glanced past her soft, white shoulder*
> *and saw death . . . grinning.*
> *Had he come for her,*
> *Or me?*
>
> *J.*

Again, nothing more. No address, no phone number, no way to contact him. Nothing to indicate that anything might be wrong, except for the darkness of the poem. And my name and the J. were typed. I hadn't really noticed it before. Why weren't they hand-written too?

Then the long-dormant green thing that lives somewhere deep in my digestive tract stirred into life, wrapped a tentacle around my stomach, and squeezed. A rush of dark green fear entered my psyche. Why did he need me? Was he simply down on his luck and in need of a little financial assistance? And if that was the case, why not contact our accountant, demand secrecy, and claim his rightfully due royalties? But then I realized: The accountant couldn't legally justify a transfer of funds. So the Poet had to turn to me. It was possible that I was the only one he could trust who had the funds to help him. His French friends didn't have any money. His other band-mates had the money but, perhaps, not the will to silence that he would require. After all, his letters to me were only signed "J." So whatever was going to happen was going to be on the q.t.—*if* money was the problem. I prayed that it was, and not something more serious.

The first thing I had to do was find out about the Seychelles. Where exactly were they? How many islands? What was the capital? What language did they speak—Hindi, English, a Madagascar Creole patois, Arabic . . . what? I went to a travel bookstore and asked for everything they had on the Seychelles. What they had was one book, but that was enough. It told me everything I needed to know.

Creole, French and English were spoken. That explained at least one of his attractions to the Seychelles: He could communicate in English. Not like Paris, where he couldn't even talk to a man on the street or a taxi driver, or order a meal. He had been helpless in Paris, the word-man unable to make himself understood, unable to speak to anyone. Virtually mute, he could only scream out his rage and defiance. I had thought that that affected him terribly. And the booze, of course; the mute agony embalmed by booze, and he was dead. Throw some white powder—*la Chinoise blanche*—into the toxic mix, and he was dead. Or so I had once thought.

As I read on, I found that the tiny archipelago of one hundred and fifteen islands had first belonged to the French. Later it became a British colony (appropriately, the Poet's ancestral blood ties were English). It finally became an independent republic in the Commonwealth in 1976. Its population was approximately 75,000 people, within an area of no more than one hundred square miles. The capital was Victoria, on Mahé Island.

And it was all beautiful. A tiny paradise five degrees south of the equator and remote from the rest of the world. A place where a man could disappear. However, I was sure that *someone* in the Seychelles would know the American man. But I couldn't describe him now. Was he fat, thin, gray, bald? And what name was he using? Surely not his own.

I thought I would ask for a gentleman of a certain age. Intelligent, good-mannered, a writer—an American—perhaps with a tendency to drink. Hopefully someone would know of such a man. But who to contact?

The American embassy, of course. Well . . . America does not maintain a political representation in Seychelles. 75,000 people on an archipelago somewhere due east of Mombassa do not get an American embassy.

So I called the Seychelles's travel office in New York City.

"I'm looking for a friend," I said to the woman on the other end of the line. I didn't use any real names. "I haven't seen him in many years, but I have reasons to believe he's on one of the islands of Seychelles. He's over fifty, about six feet tall, an American and a writer. He may have been living there for the better part of twenty-five years now. He had a penchant for drink, which he may or may not have today. Does any of this sound like someone you might have heard of?" As soon as I asked the question I realized how absurd it all sounded. How could she, or any one at the travel office possibly have any knowledge of the Poet?

"I'm sorry sir, that description doesn't fit anyone I know. I'll ask here at the office, but we do get a lot of tourists these days and it's really quite impossible to keep track of them all." She was pleasant, and seemed genuinely concerned, but stumped.

"Thank you," I said. "Could you please send me everything you have? Brochures, maps, a list of hotels, bars, anything and everything. Whatever information you have. Please?"

"Of course," she said. "May I have your name and address?" I gave her a phony name and my accountant's address.

"I'll call them all if I have to," I said.

"Sir? Might I suggest that you *go* to the Seychelles. It would be so much easier. Our phone system is not the best. And it would be a *marvelous* vacation for you. You'd love it there. As your friend does, if he's been there for twenty-five years."

The packet from New York arrived in two days. I leafed through the lushness of the brochures and was mesmerized. What a delightful string of islands and what a quaint, laid-back way of life. Beach-front hotels, tiny shops, gourmet restaurants, tropical bars, scuba diving, nature preserves—my kind of place, and just the place for a refugee from the '60s. The Poet as beachcomber.

And then the next letter came.

> *Roy:*
>> *I see the unseen.*
>> *I touch all things.*
>> *I create the course of*
>> *the stars and*
>> *of all nature.*
>> *I am the light. I can be anywhere*
>> *in space and time. I can be life*
>> *and death and life.*
>> *I can.*
>> *I AM.*
>
> *Gauguin*

I loved the poem, and I understood the clue, too. He didn't type "J." He was emulating Paul Gauguin. He was doing his own escape to paradise to perfect his art, uninvolved with the daily problems of Los Angeles life. Uninvolved with rock-and-roll stardom. Hell, uninvolved with Western civilization itself. And I remembered that we had once stood on the beach of El Segundo, California, with the shore break lapping at our feet, and come to the realization that we were at the end of the West. The terminus of the Western dream. The very end of Western civilization.

So, like Gauguin, he had fled the whole thing. But the Poet had tossed in a Harry Lime. This was The Third Man. A dead man not really dead. A grand con. A classic swindle. He had pulled a rabbit out of his hat and jumped in to take its place.

And when Orson Welles, in his *own* magic show, turned the top hat upside down, why it was empty! The Poet was gone. And we all wept for him. And our tears were applause for the efficacy of the illusion.

But like Harry Lime, the Poet seemed to be returning. I assumed he was in trouble—why else would he come back out of the trick hat? And that was my question to answer.

The next day I made the inevitable decision. I would go to the Seychelles. I would scour those little islands . . . and I would find him.

2

I called my travel agent the next day and booked the flight. British Air from Los Angeles to London, London to Nairobi, Nairobi to the Seychelles—nearly twenty hours of flying. Far too long. But what awaited at the destination would perhaps be a dream come true.

I was leaving in a week. I desperately wanted my wife, Dianna, to come. But she had to stay behind to take care of our two children, who were at that awkward, early-adolescent phase of first rebellion and testing. We talked about her coming with me, but she thought it best to stay home and be the authority against which the kids could practice their budding independence.

"You really don't know how long you'll be there, Roy," she said. "It could be a few days or a few weeks. There's no way of knowing. I just can't leave the children for an unknown length of time. And besides, I'm still not convinced it's real. I don't want to go halfway around the world searching for a dream that may be so much smoke."

I kissed her forehead. "It would be a great vacation though. We could be Adam and Eve in paradise. Evidently there's an old legend that says the Seychelles are the original Garden of Eden. All we have to do is find that little deserted beach, take our clothes off, and . . . "

"I know, begin the world again," Dianna said as she pressed herself against me. "Like we did in Baja when the whole band went down to that little fishing resort. The beaches were so beautiful, and so deserted. We went off on our own, remember?"

"How could I forget? Walking in that sand, naked. The water was so warm and soft." And I remembered her in my arms, pressed against me, skin to skin, feeling the heat of her body as it opened to mine. "You were so warm and soft."

"That was beautiful, wasn't it? I'd never made love outdoors before."

"We could do it again in the Seychelles, you know. In fact I guarantee we will do it again in the Seychelles."

She smiled at me, put her hand on the back of my neck and gently pulled my head to her parted lips. "Why don't we do it now," she said. "The children won't be home for a couple of hours. Let's imagine we're in Baja again."

We kissed and I lifted her off her feet and carried her into the bedroom. And we were in Baja, again.

Dianna and I had been together since before the band. We met in college, the year before I met the Poet. She was there from the beginning. From the first tenuous steps of our song-writing, the finding of the drummer and the guitar player, the endless rehearsals and perfection of our music, the rejections by all the record companies in Los Angeles, the gigs on the Sunset Strip at which the Poet began the creation of his public persona: the "Snake Man." Our eventual signing with the record company from New York. The recording of the first album and the rise of our single to the number one spot in America. Top of the charts! We had made it. And Dianna was there, at my side, for all of it.

She was my other half and she was the band's muse. She encouraged us, supported us, stimulated our imaginations and even fed us when necessary. She saw the potential in the Poet long before anyone else did. Our friends from college thought it was an absurd idea: a rock band with the Poet as the lead singer? Ridiculous! "Why, he's just an immature punk," some of them said. "You'll never amount to anything, Roy. He sucks." But Dianna and I knew that what we were creating was authentic. The band had it—that elusive "it." We were able to seize the energy of the moment and hold it captive to our wills.

Dianna was there as we raced through our career. Album after album, concert after concert. A mad rush of creativity. A time of delight, filled with the intoxication of success. Unfortunately, the Poet also became intoxicated. With himself, and with the bottle. It was his undoing, his tragic flaw. He began to drink more and more as our success grew. Each new album seemed to increase his alcohol consumption. And his personality underwent a transformation, from young visionary to besotted lout. When we first put the band together he was a bright, charming and exciting young man. A poet of depth and perception. His words were exhilarating. Dianna and I were both in love with his stanzas. His turns of phrase were unique and took us to places no rock poet had gone before.

And we loved him as a human being. He was the young prince of America, the culmination of the destiny of this country: the merging of the Cowboy and the Indian. He was a well-born, educated white boy with the soul of a Native American. He loved the earth. His philosophy was both linear/Western and circular/primitive. He had married the opposites. And Dianna and I had never known anyone like him, before or since. And we loved him.

The Poet had been just the man to be a leader of our new movement of love and respect for the soil of our country. Out of our Native American roots would come the rebirth of the American Dream. And the Poet would lead us because he was the synthesis. He was the new gold of America fired in the alchemical alembic. He was the first step into the 21st century, the new time, which would be symbolized by the merging of art, science, and religion. He was the Cowboy and the Indian. And he would lead us.

Unfortunately, that dream was never to materialize. The Poet lost himself in alcohol and our dream died abruptly with him in Paris.

But none of that mattered anymore. The Poet was alive! At least I believed he was. And all that remained for me to do was to place my hand in the wound on his side, as St. Thomas said.

But how would I find him once I got to the Seychelles? How would I search out the American writer? All I could do was place myself in the hands of the fates.

So after Dianna and the children hugged and kissed me at the Mayor Tom Bradley International Terminal at LAX, I boarded my British Air flight for the first leg of my journey into what I hoped was not absurdity and smoke.

I settled back into the good English leather seat, got my magazines at the ready, slipped off my shoes, wrapped my feet in the little terry-cloth booties that came in the courtesy kit, and the 747 attacked the runway, roaring. We raced down the tarmac, heading due west, then rose up into the air and out over the Pacific. We passed over Catalina Island, where my son and I had gone scuba diving as a final test before certification in our PADI diver-training course. We had had a wonderful time in the California kelp beds and I looked forward to more diving adventures with him. Maybe we would start making regular trips to the Seychelles. Maybe even to dive with the Poet—he had been a swimmer in high school and perhaps now he was a scuba diver. The water in the Seychelles looked absolutely crystalline from the photos in the brochures. And the undersea life in that clear azure was amazing. I couldn't wait to slip on a tank and a pair of fins, put the regulator in my mouth and submerge into the Garden of Eden's tropical reef.

At that instant, the jumbo jet began a hard left bank over Catalina, back over the coastline of southern California and I looked down to see the little beach town of El Segundo—our home base for the beginning of our assault upon Olympus. El Segundo was where we had perfected our craft and dreamed our dreams as the five of us—the Poet, the drummer, the guitar player, Dianna and I—walked along that broad, sweeping beach of the bay of the City of Angels.

And those angels had certainly seemed to be with us in our initial burst of creativity. The music came rushing out of our fingers as if the band had tapped into some underground wellspring of inspiration. And the Poet just kept producing page after page of allegorical lyrics that took us on mythic journeys around the sun, or into the heart of darkness. We were touched by tongues of fire in the little El Segundo beach house that we used as our rehearsal space. Dianna and I lived there and the band all chipped in for the rent. We were young and alive and vital. I don't know if we've ever been so happy again.

We worked during the sunlight hours. Our schedule was usually noon to five. We couldn't rehearse after six o'clock for fear of disturbing the neighbors' dinners. It is ironic to me that we are considered to be a band of profound darkness when our songs were created in the clear, warm daylight on the crescent beach of the Bay of Angels. I always felt that a glow of sunlight infused our music even when our explorations took us into the dark zones of forbidden revelations. As the Poet entered oedipal areas of his mind, we were right with him, creating music that acted as the underpinning, the support and foundation to his plunges into his psyche. But the light was always with us. The sand and the ocean were always with us. Everything we did was permeated with the nature that lay directly outside our rehearsal room window. When we needed a break, we would walk out the front door of our old California beach house and onto the sand. Almost fifty yards of sand. A fine and broad beach, soft and golden. And then the water: the Pacific Ocean. The endless ocean that stretches seemingly forever around the globe until it finally stops at the shores of the Orient. We were at the end of the Occident, and we knew it.

We walked along the shore break and kicked water into the air, watching it become scattered diamonds in the light of the setting sun—glistening for just an instant, a tantalizing but ungraspable wealth that existed for a heartbeat—and then fall back into its watery, elemental state. It was a perfect metaphor for the transience, the impermanence of fame and fortune. "Do you want money?" the Poet would ask as we walked. "Here . . . here's diamonds for you." He would kick at the water and create a spray of diamonds. "Catch them. Quick! Put them in your pocket. Here's all the wealth you could ever ask for." And he would kick out another torrent of diamonds from his feet. They would rise into the air, exist for an instant, and then fall back, water into water. "Do we need more than we have right now?" he would ask. "We have our music, we have each other, we have our father the sun, and our mother the ocean. We have gold at our feet and more diamonds than we could spend in a thousand lifetimes. What more do we need?" And the guitar player—always the pragmatist—would say: "Well, a hit single sure would be nice." And we'd all laugh and splash him with diamonds. And then a silence would descend upon us and we would be filled with awe at the infinite blue of the sky and the almost indistinguishable blue of the ocean as they met at the horizon, the gateway to Asia. And the Poet would say: "If we could part that horizon line, lift the sky like a curtain and lower the ocean, we could see China. We could maybe, if we were lucky, see the whole world." And we would stare at that line—the meeting place of the infinite and the terrestrial—our minds wandering out and up into the air in a kind of rapture.

And then we'd have a taco. It was all we could afford. A couple of tacos and a soft drink. If we had any money from one of our few-and-far-between gigs, we'd spring for a plate of chili Colorado and a beer at Pancho's Family Café, the Poet's favorite restaurant. Sop up all that good sauce with some warm tortillas, finish off all the rice and beans, down every last chunk of Pancho's succulent beef, and wash it all back with a cold Mexican beer. That was good eating. Rosario Carillo, or Pancho, as he liked to be called, was a genius with Mexican food. The good, honest, ranchero food of cowboy Mexico: *enchiladas, tacos, frijoles, chili rellenos, cocido, arroz, galina en caldo, burritos,* and Tecate, Corona, and Dos Equis beer. The food of countless cowboy movies set near the border of Texas and Mexico. I had loved watching them eat that food, that exotic food, when I was a kid growing up in Cleveland. I always wondered what the real thing would taste like. I was sure it wouldn't be anything like those frozen TV dinners that passed for Mexican food in my youth. And there I was in California, with my girl, and my band, and we were all at our favorite Mexican restaurant eating the best Mexican food I have ever had. We were in *The Wild Bunch,* or *One-Eyed Jacks.* We were living a fantasy. And it was good to be alive.

All we had to do to complete the fantasy was to become a successful rock band. And that was not far off in the future. But the madness, the chaos and disorder, they also were not far off in the future. But what did we know of such pitfalls in those early days of dreaming and creating in El Segundo? How could we possibly have known of the decadence that awaited us in New York City? We were innocents, naïfs, and we had yet to confront the beast that lay dormant in each of us. That lustful, rapacious, greedy monster would make his appearance at the New York nightclub called Circe. We performed there for a month, just before the release of our first record. What doors of debauchery opened themselves to us in that great metropolis. Most of all for the Poet. He fell in with the artist Andy Warhol, who kept a stable of smart young things at his downtown loft— the Factory—where he produced art of a fey and passionless sort. It was flat and ironic, actually illustrator's art. But it sold well and Andy was an international celebrity, famous for his effete manner and his tousled white wigs. The motto at his Factory may well have been "All sins are permitted here," based on the stories and rumors that circulated about the goings-on in his cavernous loft space.

And the Poet took to it with abandon. After all, he was an explorer, a seeker after sensations. And at the Factory he was able to indulge his wildest imaginings. Andy loved the West Coast wild man, encouraging him to take more risks, to indulge in more pleasures. And the Poet obliged. But the price of that wanton world of lust was the gradual loss of his soul. It happened slowly, but inexorably. Over the course of the next few years we watched his metamorphosis from golden promise into a darkened, self-indulgent rock star.

But his poetry never suffered. In spite of his new lifestyle, the poetry remained his one link with the creative explosion of energy we had all experienced on the beach of the Bay of Angels. He never lost the ability to turn a phrase. He never lost the probing, searching, multilayered word play, for which I loved and respected him. I could forgive him any transgression because of those words. They were what brought us together in the first place and they remained a constant source of wonder to me until the day he died. I could put up with all of his ridiculous friends and their attitudes. I could tolerate any of his transgressions, any of his alcohol-induced meanness, just so long as the words kept coming. And they did. His Wild Turkey consumption never seemed to interfere with his creativity. He became the classic drunken poet. I had read them, knew the literary tradition of wild man/poet, but had never had to live with one, day to day. And *that* was a bitch.

The Poet's personal decline was especially hard on the guitar player and the drummer. They were not exactly literary types, and consequently had no elevated beatnik framework in which to place our drunken lead singer. They did not see him

as a latter-day Rimbaud, or the next in line for Kerouac's man-
tle. To them he was a drunk and they could not tolerate his
increasing excesses. I think the hardest part for them was the
wild mood swings. We never knew when the *nasty* would
make his appearance, because most of the time the Poet was
the same fellow we had known on the beach, the same friend
we had put the band together with, the same rich-voiced
singer we had created our songs with. But some of the time he
was his own evil twin. And that creature, that alter-ego
dybbuk was unbearable. When he was Hyde it was impossible
to be with him.

I was powerless to stop the inevitable. I knew that the eventual end of his drinking would be his death. In a DWI automo-
bile accident, or falling out of a window, or hit by a car while
staggering across a busy street, or beaten to death by a group of
outraged Chicanos or African-Americans after he threw some
racial epithet in their faces. Testing them, testing the limits, testing himself. I had seen him do it. It was only a matter of time
until something mortal happened.

But I was never able to grasp the psychological problems he
was wrestling with. It was impossible for me to understand how
a young man could be an alcoholic. In those days I thought
alkies were all middle-aged and older bums. Skid row derelict
winos drowning on the corner of Fifth and Main in downtown
L.A. How could a rock star of twenty-five be an alkie? He had
everything. We had realized our dreams of El Segundo; dreams
of art and music and records and tours and fame and *mucho
dinero*: we were *there*, rock Olympus. And as we climbed to the
pinnacle he drank more and more. I had no idea why, and I had
no idea how to stop him.

The 747 was now over the Midwest and it was time for our

microwaved meal. I ate a few bites of mystery fish, settled back with a glass of California chardonnay and let my thoughts revolve through a Möbius strip of images. And I remembered our confrontation with the Poet. An encounter session in which the guitar player, the drummer and I told him he was drinking too much and we could see it affecting his health. We verbalized it for him, bringing our thoughts out into reality. We didn't want him to think he was fooling us or hiding it from us, and we didn't want to allow him that kind of secret space. It was the hardest thing we ever did, confronting our friend that way. But we loved him and wanted him to be the prince again, not the reprobate he had shape-shifted into.

We were on to him and he now knew it. It had been spoken aloud, in plain words. And he hung his head, ashamed, and said: "I know. I know I'm drinking too much. I'm really trying to quit." That was all we needed to hear. We had confronted him, he had acknowledged the problem, and he was going to do something about it.

Well, how naive of us. He didn't stop and he didn't appear to be trying to stop. He didn't stop until it all caught up to him in Paris. And then he stopped living—the ultimate cure for an alcoholic. He was buried and that was the end of him—but not the end of his legend. His death in Paris was the beginning of the mythology of the Snake Man. The press had called him that, and the hoi polloi and the writers loved that sobriquet. He represented all the dark twistings and turnings of the repressed desires of the public. He came to represent primordial urges, the seductive serpent of the Garden of Eden. Sexual license.

And now my goal was to find him. I was hurtling over the continent, headed toward a remote set of islands in the Indian Ocean in the hope that Dionysus was still with us. It was absurd, but it was possible. And I was not going to let the possibility slip away.

My thoughts wandered off and I saw him, once again, on stage. All wild and leather-clad, dancing in his unique American Indian/shaman style. We would drive him into a frenzy. The guitar player, the drummer and I would flail away at our instruments, pushing him to ecstatic heights. And he was the leader of the audience's journey. Twenty thousand people following his every move, absorbed in his words, transported by the music that underpinned the entire evening's seance. For that is what our performances became: seances. But not to *summon* the dead—rather to palliate the dead and allow us, the living, to celebrate our lives free of ghosts. We explored the dark corridors and passageways of the evening's collective unconscious, and then exploded into the light. Into the sheer joy of existence, with the Poet doing his best satyr's stomp, freeing the audience from the chains of society's restraints. We had opened the gates of purgatory and allowed the wild children to leap out and dance around the bonfire on the hillside, led by the electric shaman and his rock band. The night became primitive, pre-Christian and very cathartic. Most of all, for the Poet.

Which is probably why he never missed a performance, save one. In spite of his drinking, he was always ready to rock. Nothing could keep him off the stage. I think he actually lived for those rituals of ours, those electric seances that were called concerts. He never seemed quite so alive as when he was leading us all on our ceremony of self-discovery. What revelry, what intoxication. Performing on stage with him was, as we used to say, the best part of the trip. Nothing could compare to a gathering of the tribe and the immersion into the electric tribal rite of that golden age of rock music. And it was happening all over the country, all over the world. Europe was on fire. England started it all with the Beatles and the Rolling Stones, and it spread around the globe.

And there I was, flying along the curve of that globe at a speed almost beyond sound, on a quest to find the Poet in his remote, tropical hideout. I could not contain my excitement at the prospect of his actually being alive, of being able to see him again, to talk to him. I needed to hear his words again, to hear him spin his phrases. I wanted to hear the story of his life. And to finally know the truth.

3

And then we were landing in England. Coming down into Gatwick, a sort of international transfer hub meant to relieve the congestion at Heathrow. Of course, Gatwick itself was now overcrowded, and since I had a two-hour layover before my flight to Kenya, there was nothing I could do but join the throng in the terminal. We deplaned, did customs, and I entered the United Nations general assembly. Everyone was there. The world was there. Indians, Africans, Asians and Europeans. Milling and conversing in a multitude of tongues. The tower of Babel. The citizens of planet Earth, on the move.

I just wandered among them, looking at their colorful dress

and listening to the music of their languages. The swirl and din completely engulfed me and I seemed to be in slow motion, moving through a continuously changing kaleidoscope. My thoughts went back to our band's first landing in England.

The band had come to play the Around and Around, a new light-show venue in London housed in an ancient railroad-engine turnabout. It had been modeled after the infamous San Francisco psychedelic ballroom, the Fillmore Auditorium. And, fittingly, we were to play there with the number one band from San Francisco. The West Coast had come to London. And we tore it up. They were great and we were even better. The Poet was in peak form and our performance was recorded for posterity by one of the British television production companies. It was a marvelous time for all of us, the bands *and* the audience.

It was time to board my flight to Nairobi, Kenya, the next stop on my journey into the unknown. I felt like Willard in *Apocalypse Now,* heading upriver to find Colonel Kurtz. As I settled back into my British Air leather, I remembered our other European gigs with the San Francisco band. It was in Stockholm, at a magnificent Baroque concert venue, that the Poet missed his only performance. He had spent the afternoon strolling the streets of the hippie district of the city with two or three members of the other band and consuming every drug, pill, and drink that was offered to him by the benign residents of the area. When we got to the concert hall that evening, the San Francisco band was already on stage. The Poet heard the sound and fury of their music and bounded out to join them in a bit of Dionysian improvisation. With the spotlight on him, he proceeded to sing and dance himself into a whirling-dervish frenzy. The San Francisco rockers thought his antics hilarious and accompanied his whirling by playing faster and faster. The Poet went 'round and 'round in circles, twisted himself up in the microphone cord, lost his balance, and fell flat on his face on the stage of one of Stockholm's most magnificent concert venues, usually reserved for the music of Bach, Beethoven and Brahms.

The Poet lay deathly still for a moment, then stirred, extricated himself from the clutches of the mic cord, leapt to his feet, gave the audience a gracious bow, and danced off the stage. We all applauded him and headed for our dressing room. We laughed and joked, had a Heineken or two, and then I saw the Poet lean back against a wall, beer in hand, and slowly slide down to the floor, passed out cold.

When he couldn't be roused, the paramedics were sent for. Our friends from San Francisco had finished their set and the stage was being prepared for us as our lead singer lay on the floor of the dressing room, zonked, gone. The ambulance arrived, the Swedish medics wrapped him in a rubber sheet for warmth, put an oxygen mask on his face, lifted him onto a stretcher, and carried him out the door as Quince, our roadie, came into the room and said, "We're on in five minutes, guys!"

We went on stage, the three of us, and asked the audience if they wanted their money back since our Snake Man would not be able to perform that night due to his being wrapped in a rubber sheet. The audience didn't care, they just wanted to hear music. American music. They didn't care who sang the songs. In unity they started clapping together and chanting, "Play music, play music, play music!" The guitar player and I looked at each other and shrugged. "What the hell," he said, "we'll do it."

"Sing?" I asked him.

He smiled. "Sure, we know the words."

And we did it. Quince moved the vocal mic over to stage left, the guitar player's domain (I already had a vocal mic at the keyboards), and then moved the drum riser slightly forward to center stage. And we did it! Sang and played our asses off as the Swedish audience got their nut and even sang along with us on whatever songs they knew. And the drummer was on fire. He even made the morning paper, with a picture of him maniacally flailing away at his drum kit. He looked great. And on the front page, no less. He was in heaven. It was a grand success.

The next day we went to the hospital to retrieve our lead singer. He was waiting for us in the lobby, looking perfectly fine. He had had a very sound and very long night's sleep, and was ready to rock.

"I feel great, you guys," he said. "What happened last night?" He gave us his best Cheshire cat grin. "I don't remember a thing!"

All we could do was laugh. What else could you do with him? "Come on, Jordan," I said. "We've got a gig in Denmark, tonight." And off we went, piling into the waiting limos, the four Musketeers, ready to continue our assault on the unsuspecting capitals of Europe.

I looked out the window and we were now over the Mediterranean, leaving Europe behind. And then I saw a crescent-shaped island. It looked like it might have been a blown-out volcano that had exploded and then sank, leaving only the crescent rim above the water. And then I realized it was the island of Santorini, a possible site of Atlantis, lost in the middle of the Mediterranean Sea.

And I thought of my walks on the beach with the Poet, when we discussed the possibility of this very island being the lost city—or was Atlantis a lost continent in the Atlantic, or was it in the Pacific Ocean, or was that the lost continent of Lemuria?

We had talked of Atlantis tying in with the flood legend, and of the fact that most ancient cultures had a story of a great inundation that destroyed the earth thousands of years ago. Many Native American tribes had stories of a great flood. The Hindu religion had a similar story. African tribal tales existed of a similar watery cataclysm. A Chinese legend existed. We had one in our Noah's Ark tale of God's wrath. Had Atlantis been lost in that very flood?

Or was the explosion of Santorini the reason for the fabled parting of the Red Sea, as Pharaoh's army pursued Moses and the chosen people in their flight from Egypt? Freud had suggested just such a confluence of events in his *Moses and Monotheism*, a book about the relationship of Moses and the sun-worshiping Pharaoh Akhenaten. The Poet was an avid reader of Sigmund Freud and had told me the story, as Freud dictates it, of how Moses and his people had come to a place of difficult passage. They found themselves on a peninsula of land, actually at the Mediterranean and not the Red Sea, with another peninsula jutting out a few hundred yards away. That was where they had to go, but the water was too deep to cross, and they could not turn back for Pharaoh's army was hot on their heels. At that instant a deep rumbling was heard and a great cloud of smoke appeared in the north, out over the water. The volcanic island of Santorini had exploded, and the subsequent sinking of the island had caused a crater to open in the sea floor. The waters of the Mediterranean were sucked into that great hole, including the waters blocking the path of Moses and the Israelites. Dry land now appeared in front of them and they all crossed over, and then Pharaoh's army came. At that exact instant the hole of Santorini filled with water, creating an enormous back-splash and generating a huge wave, which came sweeping out, racing in every direction across the Mediterranean. That wave hit the Egyptian shoreline just as the pursuing army entered the waterless trough the Israelites had crossed not a half-hour before. And the army was inundated. The Jews were free. And the story of the event became a parting of the sea—the Red Sea—by God.

And as the Poet and I walked on the beach of El Segundo he said, "Think of it, Roy. The possibility of such an event happening at that exact instant . . . well, could it be?"

I seriously doubted it. "I don't think the laws of probability would be working in the favor of such an event," I said.

"But," he added, "do you think it more probable that a divine entity would intrude in the events of man? Is it even possible for a divine entity to do that?"

"Of course it is," I said. "Divine entities can do anything . . . that's why they're divine."

He laughed. "Well, then one more question. Is there even such a thing as a divine entity?"

"Are you asking me if there is a God?"

"I suppose I am. Is there one God; or many, like the Greeks believed; or are there three, like the Father, the Son, and the Holy Spirit? I mean, just how many are there?"

"I don't know, Jordan. I suppose it depends on your point of view, on whether it's the same as everyone else's."

"Well, did Freud's Pharaoh, Akhenaten, have a different point of view from the other Egyptians of his time? I mean, how was *his* different from his subjects, his fellow Egyptians? He was in the same place at the same time as they were. His perspective was exactly the same as theirs, and yet . . ."

I completed his thought for him. "He tried to start a new religion, didn't he?"

"Exactly. Why?"

"He must have seen something the others didn't."

"A vision? But of what? Did he see the heavens part and God come riding down on a white charger with a host of angels around him?"

I laughed, "No, that's Jesus in his second coming. I don't think Egyptians of the 18th dynasty had visions of Jesus. Akhenaten had a solar vision of some sort."

"But it's the same sun. Our sun is the same sun the Egyptians were under 3,500 years ago. There is no difference. Look at it, that's the sun that Akhenaten saw in Egypt. Are you having a vision?"

"No, man. And I want one. I want to know what that guy in Egypt saw."

"So do I, Roy. That's exactly what I want . . . a vision."

And we stood there, basking in the sun, two young seekers, gazing out at the horizon and feeling the waves breaking softly at our feet on the far western shore of the continent.

The Poet finally spoke again. "Do you think Nietzsche had a vision?"

"I don't know. He doesn't talk about it in what I've read, but he did write *Beyond Good and Evil*. That's a concept that must have come from some kind of vision, don't you think?"

"Maybe, but I haven't gotten beyond *The Birth of Tragedy*. I love that book. The Dionysian impulse and its opposite, the Apollonian impulse. Two diametrically opposed tendencies that ultimately come together in the artist. The highest goal of our society . . . to be an artist."

"Thomas Jefferson said, about the Revolutionary war: 'I am a fighter so that my son can be a farmer and *his* son can be a poet.'"

"Exactly. They knew, Roy. The Founding Fathers knew that

the goal of America was an elevation of the human spirit. Not business, not profit. It was in every man pursuing his own happiness. And the attaining of that happiness would transform him into an artist. An artist of life."

I protested. "But we don't need a nation of poets and painters. We need brick layers, and chefs, and school teachers."

"Of course," he said. "*Life* artists . . . with each one approaching his or her life the way an artist approaches his creation."

"Sounds like pie-in-the-sky, Jordan. Almost unobtainable."

"Not if you believe, Roy. Like the Mets when they won their first World Series."

"When was that?" I asked.

"Doesn't matter, it's what they said." Then he did a comic Brooklyn accent. "'Da New Yawk Mets . . . ya gotta believe!'"

And we walked off, laughing with each other, heading along the beach to our rehearsal space, in the bright light of the sun and the enthusiastic glow of our youthful idealism.

Now, I looked out the window of our racing Airbus and we were over Egypt. And I saw the Nile, the source of all life for that desert kingdom. And I thought of Akhenaten's vision, and I wondered if the Poet had found his. And then I wondered if I would find *him*. And if I did, who would he be?

4

We touched down in Nairobi for an hour-long layover. Africans disembarked and only a scattering of passengers were in line to board for the flight out over the Indian Ocean. I milled about in the waiting area and felt the heat of Africa. It was intense and powerful. The sun seemed strong enough to darken the flesh permanently if one lived there for more than a few generations. The light in England would definitely whiten the skin—less melanin for less sunlight. And perhaps race is as simple as that—a small amount of melanin.

I bought an African edition of *Time* magazine, the *International Herald-Tribune*, and an *Africa Today* at a news kiosk; had a strong, sweet, Turkish-style coffee while standing at a counter; and then it was time to re-board for the final leg of my journey into the unknown.

The plane rose up and out over an azure sea. The water was inviting, perfect. The Indian Ocean had a unique quality. A certain softness, a look of tranquility. The perfect blue lulled me to sleep.

I awoke with a start to an announcement being made over the P.A. system. "We are beginning our final descent into Seychelles International Airport. Please fasten your seatbelts." I looked out and saw a kaleidoscope of blues and greens. Rings of coral reefs around small, granite islands changed the sea from a deep indigo to a soft turquoise and then to an even softer, almost powder blue. Little crescent beaches added an inviting gold to the palette, and that gave way to a dark and lush green—the green of the forest, the jungle, the home of the coco-de-mer.

The plane touched down at Point La Rue, virtually on the beach. There was nothing but water to our right and the rich green to our left. My journey halfway around the globe was finally over, and as I stepped out into the air of the Seychelles, I was enrobed with the perfume of flowers. The air was heavy with oxygen and the good negative ions of the sea. It felt rejuvenating, invigorating. I knew that if the Poet were here he would not be dissipated. Not in this atmosphere.

I did a quick customs check, got my passport stamped, and hailed a cab to take me into Victoria, the capital city.

It was a bustling, charming little gathering of buildings no higher than two stories. Quaint shops selling all manner of goods, outdoor market-stalls bright with fruits and vegetables, colorful homemade fabric everywhere both for sale and being worn by the locals, a silly central-square clock tower in a gaudy Victorian style, a little harbor with local fishing boats and some pleasure craft, and a racial mixture unlike any I had ever seen. The skin tones ranged from ebony to bronze to tan to cream to white.

Evidently the Seychelloise are a mixture of African, European, Indian, and Asian. They gave up racial classification sometime back around 1915—too varied to keep track.

The atmosphere was extremely relaxed. Nothing seemed rushed. The island's internal rhythm had none of the frantic tempo of modern civilization. The people moved at a languid pace, with an easy, rolling gait. It felt good to be there, good to be alive in that light. That intense, clear, brilliant light. Everything seemed more vibrant than what I was accustomed to. The sun was everywhere in Victoria. Its presence controlled the life of the town. Its radiance was the dominant factor in the Seychelles. It was the very heart of the people's existence.

The cab pulled up at my hotel, the Pension Nicole. It was small and old but it was in the center of town. I didn't want to be out on the beach to the northwest, Beau Vallon, the tourist mecca on Mahé. I knew the Poet wouldn't be out there. If he were anywhere on the island, he would be near Victoria. For one thing, he would need the bookstores that I saw—two of them— and he would need the outdoor markets, and the authenticity of town life where nearly everyone was a native Seychelloise. So I felt secure in my choice of a hundred-year-old pension in town.

And it was charming. A small lobby, all tropical hardwood, circulating fans, no air conditioning, and my room—complete with wooden shutters and mosquito netting over the bed— looked out on a small courtyard with palm trees and hibiscus flowers. Perfect Somerset Maugham.

I unpacked, hung my clothes in the carved French armoire, took a quick shower, and called Dianna.

After a quick, reassuring chat with my wife I dressed and headed out into that dazzling light, to find the Poet.

I made a right turn onto Market Street. I thought I'd try the bookstore that was close to the hotel. I didn't want to go to the police station, although that would have been the logical place to start. I didn't want to arouse the local constabulary with my questions concerning a man in his late fifties, a writer, an American. I could imagine the bureaucratic questioning. They would want to know what I wanted with this man. Was he accused of a crime?

"No, you see, we thought he was dead, but he may have actually staged *his own death. And I believe he's here, in the Seychelles. He's a friend of mine."*

"Why would he stage his own death, Monsieur, *if he has not committed a crime?"*

"No, no crime. He's a poet and he was at one time a singer in a rock band."

"And why should a singer stage his own death, Monsieur?"

"To . . . I guess, uhh, to escape from . . . "

"To escape from a crime, I would think, Monsieur."

"No, it was a long time ago. You don't understand."

"We do not harbor criminals in the Seychelles, Monsieur. Even if his crime was a long time ago, he will be brought to justice. Now, let us start at the beginning. Tell me of this man."

So the police station was my last resort. If I couldn't find the Poet on my own, only then would I turn for help to the police. But I was confident that I *could* find him soon enough on my own.

How wrong I was. For the next two days I walked the streets of Victoria, inquiring after the Poet. At the Antigone Bookstore the proprietor seemed strangely reticent, reluctant even to consider my questions. An American who might come into his shop on a more or less regular basis? "I do not know of such a man, sir." But his eyes shifted away from mine as he said it. It gave me hope that he was not telling the truth, that he perhaps had an agreement with the Poet to keep his presence on the island a secret, if anyone should inquire about him.

But in going up and down Market Street, and Revolution, Independence, Francis Rachel, 5th of June, Palm Latania, Liberation, and Bois de Rose—streets of great charm and color, streets of ornate balconies and corrugated tin roofs—I couldn't find him. I moved through the multi-racial world of Victoria, asking about the Poet to no avail. I inquired at the La Kaz shop, at Jivan's Imports on the corner of Albert and Market, at Sunstroke T-shirt shop, at little general stores like Chetty and Pillay and Kim Koon where one could buy virtually anything from a box of matches to canned meat to video cameras. I asked after the Poet at the post office, at the arts-and-crafts co-op Codevar, and at Ray's Music Room, the local CD shop that had island folk music, sega and rap music all playing at the same time in a jumble of sound that mirrored the jumble of races in the streets. They would know him here, I thought. He couldn't exist without music. But again eyes were averted, "No Monsieur, I not know such as him." And I knew I was being lied to.

I continued on down avenues of shady trees and riotous flowers, past the courthouse and the little soccer stadium. I didn't bother asking at the courthouse. But I did ask after him at the old, brightly painted, tin-can–like stores just a few steps on. Temooljes Foods, and Adam Moosa's Cloth Shop, and Chaka Bros. Hardware. I tried the National Museum, just opposite the street-craft stalls of Independence Avenue, on the odd chance that someone there might just know the Poet. The museum was both charming and ridiculous. Ancient ripple-glass cabinets displayed all kinds of oddities—pirate's pistols, stuffed birds, Seychelles musical instruments, Chinese plates and cups, giant clam shells for holding holy water in the churches, crocodile skulls, fabric flowers, the coco-de-mer, and stuffed turtles. But no one had heard of the man I described.

Then I tried the new National Library and Art Gallery. It had just opened a few years back and it was obviously the pride of the island's architects. A kind of tropical gothic with Grecian columns and block tiles. Not exactly a harmonious blend, but again, an island mixture with a character all its own. I was certain the Poet would be a patron of the library, and from the look of the woman behind the main counter, he may have been. But she wouldn't admit to it.

Had he asked these people to lie for him? The bookstore, the music shop, the library were all places that he would frequent, but I was met at each by a shift of the eye or a turning of the head when I asked after the Poet. Eventually, however, someone would slip, and I knew it.

I walked on in the capital city of paradise, questioning its populace. They were always charming, always a smile on the face and a lilt in the speech, but they didn't know of him. Or wouldn't admit to it. I walked out on Long Pier to the end of the harbor and thought of the pirates who had used the pistols in the museum. It was a fine little harbor, all clean and snug. A perfect place for ships with sails and bearded crews with larceny in their hearts. And then I went to the inter-island schooner terminal. I watched people coming and going, out to Praslin Island and La Digué, about thirty miles to the northeast. Maybe I would see him. But even if he were there, coming back from a trip to one of the outer islands, would I even recognize him? But I knew I would, by his eyes, his stride—relaxed and confident—and his very presence, his aura. I would recognize him.

I sat there, waiting for him, gazing out at the beauty of the Indian Ocean. Little puffs of clouds hovered over the sea, white and almost stationary, like frigate birds gliding on thermals. In the near distance, the islands of the St. Anne Marine National Park rested comfortably. They were a nature preserve and the prime diving spot in the Seychelles. The light and the air sent me into a reverie and I was simply alive in the moment.

But was the Poet here or was this trip one gigantic mistake? My hand drifted to my pocket. I had one of his poems with me, a talisman of sorts. Lyrics to a song we never completed. A bit of sympathetic magic to draw him to me. I unfolded the paper and read it:

> *I received an Aztec rush of vision*
> *And dissolved myself in sweet derision*
> *closed my eyes, prepared to go*
> *A gentle breeze informed me so*
> *And bathed my skin in ether's glow*

He had to be here, in this air, in this gentle breeze. And hopefully with a vision. I knew I would find him.

For two days I wandered, loving every minute of my time in paradise but growing increasingly frustrated. Where the hell was he? Why couldn't I get anyone to squeal on him? Why wouldn't they open up? Then on the third day I found myself on one of the back streets of Victoria, one of the streets heading north, up into the lush, green mountains that so beautifully ring the city. I had climbed for perhaps twenty minutes when I heard American rap music rapidly approaching from behind. I turned and three skateboarders were closing fast. They were in their early teens, barefoot, wearing baggy shorts with island-wild shirts. One of them—fair of complexion and with curly blond dreadlocks that had only just begun to grow—carried a boom box that was jabbering away over a strong and steady drum machine beat. I stepped aside to let them pass, and then I saw it. The boy with the boom box looked uncannily like the Poet! The Poet at fourteen, with dreadlocks, and some African genes sprinkled lightly into him.

"Boys, wait!" I cried out. They came to a stop and looked at me, the boom-box volume falling politely away to a murmur.

"What you want, mister?" said the shortest of the boys, in a thick island patois.

"Maybe you guys can help me. I'm looking for a man. About my age. He's a writer, a poet. An American."

"Why are you looking for him?" the boom box boy said, regarding me very seriously. His accent had only the lightest touch of the islands.

"He was a friend of mine a long time ago. We went to college together. I haven't seen him in years. I came all the way from the United States to find him."

The third boy spoke up. "You not a detective, is you, mister?"

"No son. I'm a musician."

"Maybe you play in the police band."

What an imagination. "Is there even such a thing as a police band?" I asked him, chuckling to myself.

The short boy jumped in, "Sure, mister. We gots a police band right here in Victoria. Don't you gots a police band where you come from?"

"I'm from California. I don't think we have police bands in California."

"Why not? Who march in you parades if you don't gots no police band?"

"Well, high school marching bands. And the Army band, they love to march in parades. And so do the Marines. They have a very good band."

"We don't gots no army in Seychelles. Only police. They march . . . and play pretty good, too."

"Good for them. But I play keyboards. It would be a little difficult pushing a keyboard down the street and playing it at the same time, don't you think?"

Two of the boys laughed, but the boom-box boy just stared at me, very intensely. "Sure would, mister," said the third boy, "but that don't mean you not a detective."

"Well, I'm not. I just want to find my friend. You see, we thought he was dead. But over the last couple of months I've received some letters from him. Just short lines of poetry, actually. And they've been mailed from here, the Seychelles. I've come to see if he sent them to me. If he's actually alive."

Boom-box boy smiled for the first time. "He's alive, mister. But he didn't send the poems."

My heart leapt into my throat. "What? You know him?"

"Sure, mister. He's my father."

"What?!" I sounded like a parrot, squawking. "Your father? The Poet is your father?"

"He's waiting for you . . . mister Roy."

I instinctively took a step back. "You know me?"

"My mother told me about you."

"Where is he? Please, tell me."

He smiled again. "I can't tell you. You have to find him yourself"

"Find him? How?"

"That's part of the game."

"Ohh, that's so like him. Your father, I mean."

The boy shook his head. "He doesn't even know you're coming."

"What?!"

The third boy spoke up. "You sounds like a parrot, mister. 'Whak, whak, whak!'"

They all laughed and did more parrot-squawks together. "Whak, whak, whak," flapping their arms and acting silly.

Even I had to laugh. I *did* sound ridiculous, but I had found him. Almost. This boom-box rasta-locks boy was his son! And he looked just like him, but him as a mixed-race Seychelloise. Now I just had to get him to tell me the rest of the story.

"Please, son. Tell me."

"I can't. My mother has sworn me to a secret. I can't tell a secret."

"Not one he swear to, mister," shorty said. "You gots to go confession to Père La Farge at St. Paul's if you tells a secret you swears to."

"I can give you a hint, though. That's not telling a secret, is it?"

He was just like his father. The same clever mind.

"No, son. That's allowed. You're not telling the secret."

"Well, just go on up towards the mountains and then left on Bel Air Street. He's waiting for you."

"Where?"

"You'll know."

"How can he be waiting for me if he doesn't know I'm coming?"

"I can't say anymore."

And off he went, boom box blasting again, the other two boys hot on his tail, skateboard wheels clanking on the pavement.

‹, mister Roy!" They rounded

l then left on Bel Air Street!'
ıst blue-, red-, and yellow-
ne blooming vines and potted
. Through the dappled shade
ıs. Past women in incredibly
nen in crazy shirts. Past the
ınd then I came to Bel Air.
The Bar Gauguin!
ɔne a Gauguin, yes, but more
in. The Bar Gauguin!
it. My heart began to pound
ɔ breath to calm the rush of
ugh me. I felt like I was going
elevision show. Speeding like

:ed the beaded curtain hanging
instantly was blinded by the
:ing my eyes adjust to the lack
d the bartender. I approached

?"

ıelp you?"

king for a man. An American.
"

ɔm the far end of the bar. "Roy!"
I turned and saw a man beginning to rise. For a moment I

couldn't be sure. But when the man reached his full height, I knew it was him. The Poet was alive. And he looked pretty much as I had imagined he would. Salt-and-pepper gray hair—thinning on top—no beard, in relatively good shape and dressed inconspicuously. I rushed to him and grabbed him in a bear hug.

"Jordan! You son of a bitch," I said, my eyes filling with tears.

"Roy, man! I don't believe this," he responded, hugging me back with a firm strength. I could feel the love in that strength. And the joy. "So *you're* the surprise!"

"No, man, *you* are! You're alive!"

And I pummeled his back, slapping at it, hugging him, crying and laughing at the same time. I held onto him for a short eternity. I wasn't going to let go of him this time. He wasn't going to get away again. I was ecstatic. I was actually holding the Poet. Alive. Then I realized what he said. I came back down to earth, released him from my grip, stepped back and looked into his eyes. They were blue and clear, and deeper than I had ever seen them. With a softness to them, and a kindness they had never possessed before. I could tell he was at peace.

"What do you mean, *I'm* the surprise? You're the one who's dead. How can I be a surprise if you sent me those letters?"

"What letters?"

"The poems. 'To Roy, from Gauguin.' You know."

"Sorry, man. I don't know what you're . . . ahhh, yes, that explains it. Angelique said a surprise was coming for me. I was to wait at the Bar Gauguin. Man, I've been here for three days now. What took you so long?" And he laughed. That wonderful chortle of his. And it came from deep within him. Deeper than I had ever heard it before. And it tickled me. Somewhere in my ribcage, his laugh tickled me, and warmed me.

He called back to me, "Good luck, mister Roy!" They rounded the corner and were gone.

My god, the Poet's son!

I set off at almost a run. 'Up and then left on Bel Air Street!' Past the tin roof and siding, past blue-, red-, and yellow-balconied homes and shops. Past the blooming vines and potted flowers trailing off those balconies. Through the dappled shade of takamaka trees and island palms. Past women in incredibly colorful skirts and blouses. Past men in crazy shirts. Past the throbbing life of the Seychelles. And then I came to Bel Air.

I turned left, and there it was. The Bar Gauguin!

Just like the last letter. He'd done a Gauguin, yes, but more importantly, he was *at* the Gauguin. The Bar Gauguin!

And I was standing in front of it. My heart began to pound with anticipation. I took a deep breath to calm the rush of adrenaline that was coursing through me. I felt like I was going on stage for our first network television show. Speeding like crazy.

Another deep breath and I parted the beaded curtain hanging in the doorway, stepped in, and instantly was blinded by the darkness. I stood motionless, letting my eyes adjust to the lack of light. Then I saw the bar, and the bartender. I approached him slowly, my heart racing.

"*Bonjour*, Monsieur," he said.

"Hello. Do you speak English?"

"Of course, Monsieur. Can I help you?"

"Yes, please. You see, I'm looking for a man. An American. He's a writer. A poet. And I . . ."

And then I heard a shout from the far end of the bar. "Roy!"

I turned and saw a man beginning to rise. For a moment I

couldn't be sure. But when the man reached his full height, I knew it was him. The Poet was alive. And he looked pretty much as I had imagined he would. Salt-and-pepper gray hair—thinning on top—no beard, in relatively good shape and dressed inconspicuously. I rushed to him and grabbed him in a bear hug.

"Jordan! You son of a bitch," I said, my eyes filling with tears.

"Roy, man! I don't believe this," he responded, hugging me back with a firm strength. I could feel the love in that strength. And the joy. "So *you're* the surprise!"

"No, man, *you* are! You're alive!"

And I pummeled his back, slapping at it, hugging him, crying and laughing at the same time. I held onto him for a short eternity. I wasn't going to let go of him this time. He wasn't going to get away again. I was ecstatic. I was actually holding the Poet. Alive. Then I realized what he said. I came back down to earth, released him from my grip, stepped back and looked into his eyes. They were blue and clear, and deeper than I had ever seen them. With a softness to them, and a kindness they had never possessed before. I could tell he was at peace.

"What do you mean, *I'm* the surprise? You're the one who's dead. How can I be a surprise if you sent me those letters?"

"What letters?"

"The poems. 'To Roy, from Gauguin.' You know."

"Sorry, man. I don't know what you're . . . ahhh, yes, that explains it. Angelique said a surprise was coming for me. I was to wait at the Bar Gauguin. Man, I've been here for three days now. What took you so long?" And he laughed. That wonderful chortle of his. And it came from deep within him. Deeper than I had ever heard it before. And it tickled me. Somewhere in my ribcage, his laugh tickled me, and warmed me.

"What took me so long? I've been searching Victoria for the last two days. Asking everywhere. Nobody seems to know you, or will admit to knowing you. It's like some giant conspiracy out there."

"Good!" he said. "I asked certain people not to know me if anyone came asking for me."

"So why didn't you tell me to meet you at the Bar Gauguin instead of just saying 'Gauguin' like that in your note?"

"What note?"

"The notes, man. The ones you sent me, all mysterious and cryptic."

He smiled again, flashing a quick ray of light at me. "I told you . . . Angelique."

"Who's Angelique?"

"My wife."

"*She* sent those letters pretending to be you?"

"She must have. I didn't."

"But why?"

"I have no idea. All she said was for me to wait here and a surprise would come." He punched me on the shoulder, the way a good friend does. "And you're it!"

"So your *wife* planned this whole thing?"

He nodded. "Yup. Ain't she somethin'?"

"Well from the fact that we're here, you and me, in the middle of nowhere . . . I'd say she is."

"Got a couple of kids, too."

"I saw your boy and his buddies on skateboards just down the street. He told me you were here."

"He did? Is he in on the scheme, too?"

"Well, actually, he said to just go up the street and around the corner. That's all he said, and bam . . . Bar Gauguin!"

"Yeah, he's in on it."

"He looks just like you. You as a rasta boy."

"He's trying to grow his dreadlocks. Looks pretty good on him, too."

"He's a handsome boy."

"Takes after his mother." And he smiled again.

I just stood there. Smiling back at him. Looking into those blue eyes. Those eyes that had become as deep as the sea.

"God, I'm happy to see you," I finally said.

"Me too, Roy. It's been far too long, hasn't it?"

"Then why didn't you write me?"

"I don't know. Stubborn, I guess."

"You always were." And we both laughed. "Now for god's sake, tell me the story. What happened? Where did you go? How the hell did you pull off the death thing? Have you been here the whole time?" I was starting to speed again, questions tumbling out.

"Whoa, slow down." He slung an arm around my shoulder and guided me back to his place at the bar. "Sit down, man. You look like you need something cold to drink." He called to the bartender, "Jean-Luc, *un votre specialité, s'il vous plait*. For my friend, here."

"Speak French now, eh?"

"No, man," he said. "Just a couple of words and handy phrases. Like how to ask for a *baguette* or 'Where's the *toilette*?'"

"The important stuff, huh?"

"Hey, without a loaf of bread, you're in trouble."

"Same for the *toilette*," I said.

"Maybe even more so!"

I laughed. "Well, come on, Jordan. Tell me."

"Roy, we work at a slow pace here. You can't rush things. Besides, you have to have your drink, first. Jean-Luc makes a very fine planter's punch."

"What is it?"

"Sort of like a mai tai, but it's ours. Well, actually, it's Caribbean, but since we're also a Creole nation, it somehow came here and now it's our number one cooling-off drink."

"Rum and stuff, huh?"

"Fine island fruit. Always fresh here. You'll like it."

And it came. Tall, frosty, and golden. I sipped it, and it was great. "Perfect," I said.

The Poet smiled. "Goes down nice and easy, doesn't it?"

I had another sip. "You're right. I needed this."

"In this heat? And on the trail of a mysterious disappearance? Hey, you've solved the case, you deserve a drink."

"Oh, no, I've only just begun to unravel this mystery. I've got a million questions. And goddamnit, Jordan, you're going to answer every one of them."

"Whoa, Roy, a million? I told you, you got to go real slow, my friend." Then he looked at me and whispered, out of earshot of the bartender: "Don't call me Jordan again. I don't use that name anymore."

"I *knew* you must have changed it," I said.

"I had to."

"So what's your new name?"

He sipped his drink again. "Is that your first question?"

"I don't know *what* my first question is, man. All I know is you're alive. But you're still drinking."

"Just these, in moderation. But I sure did used to put it away, didn't I?"

"You were an alcoholic."

"I *am* an alcoholic. You never stop being one, but if you're smart you stop drinking. Or at the very least you learn to control it."

"How did you manage to do that?"

He sighed, took a sip of his punch, looked off into his memory, and said, "Well, that's the story in a way. Why don't I just tell it to you. As my son says, you can just chill out and listen."

"Man, I'm ready." I smiled at him. "I've been ready since the day they buried you. Go!"

5

For the first five years here I did nothing but drink, and read, of course. There was always a new book, or a classic, or something obscure to occupy my mind between drinks. I'll tell ya, Roy, Dostoevsky can kill a lot of time."

He laughed and his face crinkled, his eyes sparkled. It was a good laugh. The laugh of a man at peace. I felt easy with that laugh, and warmed by it again.

"Dostoevsky is for those long Russian winters," I said. "The ones that last from the ides of October to at *least* the ides of March."

"The *summer* is that long here." he said. "There's nothing to do when that heat comes on except drink and read. A planter's punch and a Russian novel, and six months of swelter just races by. I love Dostoevsky—the plot twists, the philosophy, his observations on the human condition, that dark Slavic soul. Sent a chill through me, that frozen Slavic thing of your ancestry." He shuddered as if reliving a memory, a moment of ice. "No wonder people considered our music terrifying. You and that damned organ. Like Slavic death. Tim Bladd—the radio guy in L.A.—once said to me that when he heard you play the organ he always thought that someone had died!"

He laughed again but was brought up short by a cough. A loose, phlegmy cough. "Too many cigarettes," he said. I ignored his excuse . . . but it registered.

"Hey, I was just playing music that was appropriate to your words. You're the oedipal man, not me."

"Yeah," he said, smiling, "But did you have to do it with such relish?"

He had me there. "Alright, I confess, I loved the dark trips. I loved all the spooky shit. I loved the psychic games, the strangeness, the bizarre. I was born to play music to your words."

"Slavic ice, like I said."

"Southern Gothic/Carson McCullers/Tennessee Williams/Arthur Rimbaud/beatnik words. What did you *expect* me to do, white bread Beach Boys? Dave 'Baby' Cortez and the happy organ, or some kind of Sam the Sham and the Pharaohs 'Woolly Bully' stuff? Your words demanded a nightmare. A *dia de los muertos* kind of sound. Latin rhythms and the nightmare carnival of death.'

"Yeah, that was us," he said. "You still played it with an inordinate amount of glee, though. I saw your head lolling back and forth. Every concert, left to right, left to right. Always in time with the rhythm. Left to right. Left to right. What the fuck were you doing, hypnotizing yourself?"

"Trance, my man. Entering the bonding state between you and me, the guitar player and the drummer."

"We did that, didn't we?"

"I was gone. In the rhythm . . . "

"For me, nothing else existed but being on that stage," he said. "It was my world, and I was the master. I could do anything and they would love it. I could try any poetic flight, any improvisation and you guys would be behind me. If it didn't work, you'd save my ass. If it did work, I swear, you'd make me levitate. I'd float on your music."

"Those poems were *our* inspiration." I smiled. "We were just trying to take it a little higher. You know, like Van Morrison says, 'Into the Mystic'."

"I was on the Trans-Void Express. Ridin' that train, that train to nowhere."

I sipped my planter's punch. The cool and the fresh fruit and the rum all passed over my tongue, hit the back of my throat and slid happily down into my belly, warming it, as being in the Poet's presence warmed my psyche. And as I sipped I imagined that long black train racing through the night—the rhythm of the tracks, the energy, the power. It was like our music. And then I realized that we were talking just as we had on the beach of El Segundo. It was as if no time had passed. The years hadn't changed us at all. And I knew he would tell me his story, but at his pace and in his own way.

"You had that book on trance states, remember?"

"I had a lot of books," he said.

"Well, this one I still have. Shamanism in Bali, *kris* dancing in Malaysia, the Ketjak dance."

"Oh yeah, that monkey chant. Guys all in a circle going 'chak-chak-chak, chaka-chaka-chaka chak.' I loved that record."

"Remember the book?"

"No . . . why?"

"Because it's about this part of the world. The Indian Ocean. The thousand island archipelago"

"So what? You think my being here was preordained, or something? It might be simply chance."

"Nope, not chance. Not with you. It was that book that laid the seeds for this adventure of yours."

"Maybe, Roy."

He sipped at his drink. A silence hung in the air. His eyes looked off and he floated away from the bar for an instant, then: "Maybe you're right. I needed to be somewhere else. Somewhere far away . . . from myself."

I was surprised at his bluntness. He had never been so forthcoming before.

"Wait a second. What was wrong with the you that you were?"

He regarded me with a slow look, a look that went straight into me. In his youth, his eyes had darted around frantically, needing to see everything—every corner, every angle. Now they were deep and peaceful. He was no longer the Snake Man of our music days. I couldn't look into his eyes back then—too much turmoil, too much chaos, too much raw power. A strange and dark power that always made the green thing that lived in the pit of my stomach stir its tentacles, sending a shiver of fear through my body. A fear that I was inadequate, somehow less than I could be. But now, his eyes were forgiving and at rest, and I had long since lost that youthful doubt of myself that I once projected into them. Now we could look at each other as equals.

I repeated my question, "What was wrong with the you back then?"

He stretched the silence to the breaking point, and then said quietly . . .

"I was a coward,"

That one blindsided me. The Snake Man, the shaman, the wildest man in rock and roll a coward? Impossible.

"Hold it, man. You held a sold-out Madison Square Garden in the palm of your hand for four consecutive nights. You manipulated a half million people at Woodstock, for chrissake. How could you be a coward?"

He grinned his sly-boy grin that I always loved, except now it came with the complexity of lines and creases of a man in his middle age who had spent too many years in a tropic corridor. "I didn't say I was shy, Roy. Now did I?"

I laughed. "Shy you certainly weren't. But I don't get it. If you had all that power, all that control over people, how were you a coward?"

"Onstage I could do anything!" His chest swelled imperceptibly. He was proud of our music, and of himself. "The audience was mine, and you guys were always there to back me up. Hell, half the time it was the three of you that set me off. All that electricity and intensity just shot through me. It was *all* a trance. The drums would shock me off into another place. Whack, bam! And I was gone. And then the guitar would bottleneck my kundalini and I'd have to—I mean *have* to—do the snake wiggle. Turned me into a fucking reptile. And then you'd lay that mystery organ over the whole thing, washing and painting the gathering with some kind of remembrance of things past.

Ghosts from all our collective childhoods. You'd put a blue dome over the entire ceremony. And I was the eye of the hurricane. I was the center. And all power was mine."

He closed his eyes and I could see him envisioning our transcendent night at Woodstock. Half a million people under his control, caught up in our music and taken to the free space on the other side. Half a million people breaking through, breaking free of their chains. An instant in time, perhaps never to be repeated, but realized and attained at least *once* in a collective lifetime. A vision of a new American possibility.

"But that was onstage," he said, coming out of his reverie. "Off stage it was a completely different story. I couldn't face the night fears. The three A.M. wakeup-to-a-guilty-conscience examination of my faults and failings and weaknesses and wrong choices and left-hand turns when I should have gone right and bad decisions and abuses of the trust everyone had placed in me. And then there was all the weight on my shoulders to be creative, witty, profound—the *leader*—to come up with the clever phrase at interviews, the noteworthy, press-worthy, quotable line that would assure our coverage in *Time* and *Newsweek* and whatever other national rags were important back then. And then those television shows, why did *I* have to do it live? You three were just finger-synching and having a grand time goofing on network TV while I had to actually sing. 'Here's your mic, kid, stand on the X there, pay no attention to the cameras and sing your ass off.' Sure, pay no attention to the fact that millions of people all over the country are watching the number one variety show on the boob tube and we're on and it's our debut and we make it or break it, our whole fucking career, riding on what *I* do.

"It was on *me*, Roy. It was all on me. And then the funny two brothers' TV show and all the horns and strings for 'Love Me.'

ducting their pit orchestra. You
and *they* lip-synched and you
r and the guitar player finger-
;hing and joking except me. I
nch. It would look phony. Big
heels Cyclops-eye TV camera
iiss a word to the pre-recorded
the illusion and fall flat on my
pid 'Snake Man,' and I hated
Sacrifice of the Reptile,' just
out snakes, an invocation of a
n Georgia and happen to like
Vas that any reason for them to
,"

ivoking that totem animal," I

believe any charlatan."

In the hour of the wolf, I was.
and found it weak, a coward's
ll my secrets, all my mistakes,
rything I had done was a mis-
take. The more famous we became, the more mistakes I made.
That's when my drinking ramped up. Hoping the booze would
knock me out and carry me beyond that wolf's eyes. Hoping to
get through his hour without waking up to the fear. The gnawing fear that sits low and evil in the gut. That blind and pointless fear . . . of what?"

"Life itself," I offered.

He smiled, raised his eyebrows like Groucho Marx and said . . .
"And death, man." He took a long, cooling pull of his planter's

punch and continued. "That's where the fear comes from. Death. But then that's where the acceptance comes from, too."

And he looked at me, or rather, he looked *into* me, and his searching gaze actually moved beyond my eyes and into my psychic body. He dove into my secrets and into their hiding place behind my navel, at that critical juncture where the sphincter muscle tries to hold the green thing in check, to prevent it from rising up the esophageal channel to the heart energy and encircling it and constricting it with its poisonous mission: the propagation of fear, anxiety, panic attacks, and ultimately madness.

"You're keeping the beast at bay now, aren't you, Roy?"

I smiled my ease to him. "Yeah, I seem to have that monster under control, my friend. But it still extends a tentacle every now and then. And it's still green." I laughed.

He grinned, "Mine, too," he said. "Man, I wrestled with that thing every which way you can imagine. And what a tough fucking opponent it is, so many arms and it comes at you from so many angles. From your childhood, from playground bullies beating you up, from Boris Karloff as the Frankenstein monster invading your dreams and lumbering down on you with the crushing of your bones as his sole, terrifying intent. From the fear of the dark swamps and bayous where I grew up, the twisted bayous that hid the monsters of my childhood id who were always trying to get into my room at night, and into *me*. From my father's spine-numbing shouts and barks, and me acquiescing—'I'll never do it again sir. *Yes* sir. *No* sir. I'm *sorry* sir.' And of course you do it again and he hollers at you again, but louder and more terrifying, and you begin to hate him, and the green thing *loves* that hate, it feeds off that hate. And it comes at you from your mother's banshee shrieks that would

Jesus, you were having a blast conducting their pit orchestra. You had them all come up on stage and *they* lip-synched and you finger-synched and the drummer and the guitar player finger-synched and everybody was laughing and joking except me. I had to do it live! I couldn't lip-synch. It would look phony. Big fucking infernal plastic box on wheels Cyclops-eye TV camera staring at me, waiting for me to miss a word to the pre-recorded track and look ridiculous. Break the illusion and fall flat on my face. And by then I was the stupid 'Snake Man,' and I hated that. Just because we did the 'Sacrifice of the Reptile,' just because one of our pieces was about snakes, an invocation of a totem. Just because I was born in Georgia and happen to like snakes and lizards and reptiles. Was that any reason for them to call me the fucking 'Snake Man'?"

"You did too good of a job invoking that totem animal," I said. "They really believed you."

"No shit. They're too ready to believe any charlatan."

"You were never a phony."

"At 3:30 in the morning I was. In the hour of the wolf, I was. That wolf peered into my heart and found it weak, a coward's heart. Those beady eyes knew all my secrets, all my mistakes, and it got to the point where everything I had done was a mistake. The more famous we became, the more mistakes I made. That's when my drinking ramped up. Hoping the booze would knock me out and carry me beyond that wolf's eyes. Hoping to get through his hour without waking up to the fear. The gnawing fear that sits low and evil in the gut. That blind and pointless fear . . . of what?"

"Life itself," I offered.

He smiled, raised his eyebrows like Groucho Marx and said . . . "And death, man." He took a long, cooling pull of his planter's punch and continued. "That's where the fear comes from. Death. But then that's where the acceptance comes from, too."

And he looked at me, or rather, he looked *into* me, and his searching gaze actually moved beyond my eyes and into my psychic body. He dove into my secrets and into their hiding place behind my navel, at that critical juncture where the sphincter muscle tries to hold the green thing in check, to prevent it from rising up the esophageal channel to the heart energy and encircling it and constricting it with its poisonous mission: the propagation of fear, anxiety, panic attacks, and ultimately madness.

"You're keeping the beast at bay now, aren't you, Roy?"

I smiled my ease to him. "Yeah, I seem to have that monster under control, my friend. But it still extends a tentacle every now and then. And it's still green." I laughed.

He grinned, "Mine, too," he said. "Man, I wrestled with that thing every which way you can imagine. And what a tough fucking opponent it is, so many arms and it comes at you from so many angles. From your childhood, from playground bullies beating you up, from Boris Karloff as the Frankenstein monster invading your dreams and lumbering down on you with the crushing of your bones as his sole, terrifying intent. From the fear of the dark swamps and bayous where I grew up, the twisted bayous that hid the monsters of my childhood id who were always trying to get into my room at night, and into *me*. From my father's spine-numbing shouts and barks, and me acquiescing—'I'll never do it again sir. *Yes* sir. *No* sir. I'm *sorry* sir.' And of course you do it again and he hollers at you again, but louder and more terrifying, and you begin to hate him, and the green thing *loves* that hate, it feeds off that hate. And it comes at you from your mother's banshee shrieks that would freeze the oil in your crankcase—those alcohol-animated screams of domination that she could never direct at her husband and spewed out at me, instead. Me, her oldest, her first baby, the thing she was supposed to nurture, to love—her son . . . and she was screaming at me. Screaming *ice* at me. The ice from her cocktails. Her omnipresent cocktails—her manhattans and martinis and daiquiris, but mainly those highballs. Fucking soda pop and whiskey, like kids drinking cold soda on a hot summer's day . . . but now as adults splashing a little booze over those sweet soda ice cubes. Hell, eventually I had to try it. That's where my drinking comes from. 'A genetic predisposition on my maternal side,' don't cha' know."

He drained his planter's punch, saw that mine was almost finished, and ordered another round.

"Then the green thing comes at you from your body, your fear of pain. Who wants to feel pain? We instinctively shun it. We run from that anguish all our lives. That pain that lies hidden away, deep in the bone and the fiber and tissue of this fleshy form of ours. And then eventually we grow up, out of our childhood, and the green tentacles come at you from a new angle— your anxiety about *women*. Are you going to get one; if you do is she going to be the right one; if she *is* the right one are you going to be able to satisfy her; if you can't satisfy her are you maybe a homosexual; and if you are homosexual, why are you in a relationship with a woman? And then you panic about your own sexual orientation and your sexual inadequacies. 'Am I gay? Am I a queer? I look so damn pretty. Why do I look so pretty? Am I gay?'"

Our fresh drinks came and I killed half of mine in a long, satisfying pull. It was midday hot. The Seychelles had pushed up into the low 90's, and this Somerset Maugham bar had no air

conditioning. The slowly turning ceiling fans didn't cool anything; they only circulated the thick, moist, tropical air; they
merely shuffled the steam. It was *hot* in the Bar Gauguin—like
that Georgia swamp, that Okefenokee that he took me to when
we played his hometown of Savannah. How he loved that
inhospitable, muck-bottomed sea of clotted vegetation. It was
completely unsuited for human habitation but the fauna loved
it. Animals, birds, fish . . . and most of all bugs. Those creatures loved it and they wanted to be there. It was like New
York City for beasts. And *he* loved it. And that's why he could
take the midday heat of the Seychelles. He was a swamp dog
at his core.

Then the quick gulp of the iced planter's punch hit me hard
somewhere behind my forehead, back in my skull. I had to close
my eyes and let the rush of pleasure/pain run its quick course.

The Poet laughed when he saw my mute agony. "Watch out,
man, don't gulp that punch. It's too potent and it'll sneak up on
you like a water moccasin coming out from under a tangle of
mangrove roots. And then you'll be bitten on the ass, fall off the
barstool, and I'll have to drag you back to your hotel room and
that wouldn't be seemly. We're adults now. We don't need to get
wasted anymore. We have to finish out these lives of ours with
some decorum, some dignity. We can't be dragging our almost-
old asses through the capital city of the Seychelles Islands like a
couple of reprobate, alcoholic ex-rock stars, now can we?"

The Poet smiled at me and continued . . . "And besides, I'm
sort of known by people around here and they'd run right to my
wife and tell her of her husband, half drunk, dragging an
American friend through the streets of Victoria like a bum, like
a rummy, like the alky that he used to be when he first came
here. Angelique would kill me."

Finally I could speak; the wave had subsided. "Strong drink," I managed to say.

"Strong enough to start a car."

"Sure is," I nodded. "But there's one thing, Jordan . . . "

"Hey, Roy," he said, putting his finger to his lips. "Shh, no 'Jordan'."

"Sorry, man, I forgot. It won't happen again."

He winked at me. "It better not. I don't want to confuse these people into thinking I'm somebody else."

I laughed. "So now you've got a wife, you're married. You're happy with a person of the opposite sex. How did you ever think you were gay?"

"Didn't you? Didn't you ever go through a period when you questioned your sexual orientation?"

"No . . . not really," I said.

"Well, I did. All those chicks . . . I couldn't satisfy them all. It was *impossible*. And it went even deeper than that, into the coiled DNA of this WASP boy. Homosexuality is always a possibility to the WASP. It's his greatest fear. That and cowardice."

I protested. "But we're all cowards, if by coward you mean afraid. It's the price we pay for being human."

"Sure, we both know that, now. But as a 29-year-old, I was ashamed of myself. I was drowning, Roy. Drowning in my own shame. I was a disgrace to myself. I couldn't tolerate our success."

He looked at the bottles of rums and cognacs and French aperitifs behind the tropical hardwood bar of the Bar Gauguin and then he looked at me, into my eyes. With that deep, straight-on stare that was part of the new Poet.

"I couldn't handle it, man. I just couldn't handle our fame, knowing I was a coward. Knowing I didn't *deserve* the fame. So

I debased myself. In an attempt to keep it going, to keep our dream going, to keep the band going, I tried to blot out my shame with alcohol."

He held up his moist, beaded glass. "With this, this liquid forgetfulness. This liquid *courage*. This divine intoxicant of the gods. Bacchanalian fuel—fuel for the orgy. Fuel for the plunge into licentiousness. Into debauchery. And it worked! The alcohol *did* make me forget. I couldn't remember who I was after a certain point. That little switch was thrown. Paul Newman's character in Tennessee Williams's *Cat on a Hot Tin Roof* talks about that switch. Except he can't throw it anymore. He just keeps drinking and drinking and Big Daddy asks him why he drinks so much and Newman tells him he's trying to flip the switch. Big Daddy says, 'What switch?' and Newman tells him about the switch in his head that turns on when he drinks enough. Way back, deep in the brain, and with enough alcohol you can flip that switch, and like magic everything is all right. The demons are gone. They don't circle your head anymore, squealing and howling their obscenities. Their fucking accusations."

He waved his hand in front of his face and then around his head as if he were shooing away flies. Except the Poet wasn't brushing away insects, he was chasing away demons. His demons. For an instant, he was battling his possessors again. They had been conjured up by his reminiscences with me and were seeking control of his psyche. They squealed and screamed at him—I could see it in his eyes—but they had no power over him, not anymore. He now had the will to resist them. Their racket fell on deaf ears and he dismissed them with a wave of his hand.

How had he gotten to this point of control? That was the question I asked myself. How had he become this new man, seemingly free of the anguish and turmoil of the days of our youth, and seemingly fully in charge of his destiny? This secure, warm man that made me glow with happiness as I sat beside him in a lazy Creole bar on a small outcropping of Eden-like islands in the middle of the Indian Ocean. How had he done it?

He continued . . . "And that's exactly what the alcohol did for me. Unlike Paul Newman's character, I could always flip the switch and get that crazy, drunken happiness. My inadequacies didn't matter. My cowardice was replaced by the will to power of a raging bull. I was the master of myself and of any situation I found myself in. I had courage and I tested it constantly. I had the courage to be a boor, to tell people what I really thought of them, to pierce their facades—their oh-so-carefully constructed shields of defense—which protected them from the outrages of life. Well, *I* was now the outrage. I was the hellhound on their trails. I became the beast of *their* fears. I could see right through them and I tore away their defenses . . . and I nailed them. Right to the cross of their own inadequacies. And then I let them hang there. In the unveiled, the *spoken* truth of their inferiority. I knew their flaws, I knew what they were hiding . . . and, I . . . "

"And you hurt them, didn't you?"

"I had to, Roy. I had to throw it all back on them before they nailed me. They all wanted to reveal my secrets. I could see it in their eyes. They were all after my soul. They wanted to possess me. And I couldn't have that. I was the Snake Man and I ruled my den. And so I leapt on their psyches and spoke the unspeakable. I shamed them.

"It was like living in a jungle. I had to fight these daily battles with people just to stay alive. I was the king onstage, but off that peacock throne . . . it was a battle of the wills. A battle for supremacy. And alcohol was my armor. The alcohol was my tempered steel broadsword. And the others, the enemy, had only thin little epees. How inadequate they were. I lopped their fucking heads off."

"They came to you with love, you know. They only wanted to bask in the glow of your success, your fame."

"That may have been true. But back then I saw them as challengers, or fools. They came to parry with me or they came to slobber on me. Either way, I had to defend myself. So I drank and I lopped off their heads."

"Sometimes you pierced their hearts. You pierced mine, and you pierced my wife's, too. I hated you for that."

He reached out a hand and then drew it back. "God, I'm sorry. I didn't mean to, amigo. It wasn't me doing it. It was the squalling brat that hid down in my belly. The brat that blocked all my decency. That nasty little homunculus." He placed his hand over mine and squeezed it ever so slightly, seeking forgiveness. "Please, tell Dianna how sorry I am. You're still together, aren't you?"

"Of course. Could I find someone better than her?"

He smiled. "Hell, no. She's your woman. She made you what you are."

"A better man than I was, that's for sure," I said, smiling back at him.

"Hell, she made us *all* better. If she hadn't been there working to support us as we created our music . . . "

"And goofed off on the beach."

"Yeah," he laughed, "great goofing on the beach. Well, the band never would have happened without Dianna, our muse."

"And even knowing that, you hurt her."

"Please Roy, it wasn't me. It wasn't the man you're sitting with now. It was an overindulged, pampered, coddled, bootlicked, fawned-over asshole. The fact is I never could have done it without you. You gave me the belief in myself, the *cojones* to actually sing on stage. Man, I was terrified when we first started. You made me feel like I could really do it, really go all the way."

"I believed in your talent. I know a good poet when I read one, and you were a good poet. And your songs were even better. They just needed a cool, jazz-rock keyboard man to bring them to life."

"But nobody else heard it. Only you and Dianna. You supported me, nurtured me . . ." He hung his head in penance. "And I hurt you."

"Hey, forget it. It was a brat from the past. He died. He got what he deserved and they buried him in Paris."

The Poet laughed, relieved. The moment of shame had passed and he was at his ease again.

"What did I say that hurt Dianna?"

"Don't you remember?"

"Hell no. I couldn't even remember what happened the night before."

"I always wondered why you wouldn't just pass out. You'd drink and drink, sucking it down like you were trying to quench some awful fire in your belly, and you would never pass out."

"Hey, I did. I passed out plenty of times. You just had to hang with me until three or four in the morning. You were always gone home by midnight. The real run didn't get started till after twelve."

"I'm glad I missed it. Somehow, none of it seemed like fun to me."

"No shit. It was pure desperation."

He looked up at the slowly turning fans, sighed, and rotated his glass as beads of moisture condensed on its surface.

"So what did I say to Dianna to hurt her?"

I sipped my drink, slowly this time. "We were at the studio, Dianna was with me, and you had your support team—your drinking buddies, Tom, Mike and Dog. Dianna and I were standing off to the side, I had my arm around her. She was holding me with both arms around my waist. We were listening to a playback. It didn't quite have it. We had to do another take. You said you liked it, and your yes men all agreed with you. I said I didn't. I said we should try it again. Then you turned to the direction of my voice. You looked at me and then you looked at Dianna—she remembers your eyes as being cold, and maybe even evil, like a shark's, unfeeling, uncaring—you saw our body posture and you said to her, to me . . . 'You're just two lonely people, clinging together.' And then you turned away, back to Tom, who had offered you another drink. I felt Dianna's energy slide out of her. She released her arms from around my waist, embarrassed, and let them hang emptily at her sides. She slumped back against the wall. You just carried on with your buddies, drinking and laughing. You didn't care that you had cut into her spirit—and you knew how sensitive she was. And you didn't care that you hurt me."

I grew angry with him, reliving that moment of anguish. Those mind games. "Shit, man," I said. "We're all fucking lonely. It's the goddamned human condition. You're damned right we were clinging together! She was my refuge. I was her support. We had found each other and we had become a unit. A single entity to ward off the chill of the night. You understand?"

"I understand," he said. "And I stand accused."

"You know what I wanted to say to you back then? As I looked over at you and Tom and Mike and Dog. You and your buddies, your laughers. You four . . . guys. I wanted to say, 'Hey, at least we're of opposite sexes!'"

And there it was. I had said it. And as soon as it left my lips I wished I could have called it back. I didn't want to hurt the Poet *now*. But I would have loved to have said it then.

The Poet stared at me in silence. "I'm glad you didn't say that back then," he said finally. "It would have destroyed me. To have that fear spoken out into the air like that, in my over-intoxicated state, I might have killed myself that very night. That was one of my biggest fears, and you would have pinned it. Right then and there, in front of everybody. Shit, Roy, I might have offed the Snake Man that night."

"You *did* kill yourself, remember?" I laughed before it could get any heavier. I had thrown off my bile, I was free of it and it was now going to fester on him. But I laughed before it could attach itself and the sound of my laughter brushed it off his shoulders, onto the floor, where it simply melted away. "That's exactly what you did."

He laughed, too. His boyish smile lighted his features. "You're right, I did . . ."

"And I want to know about it, I said."

"It's not that big a deal. Quite simple, really. But that's not the important thing . . ."

"What is?"

"Tell Dianna, when you get back, how very sorry I am for say-ing that. I love her, too, you know."

"I know. I'll tell her. But aren't you coming back with me?"

"For what?"

"Well . . . to make music. Don't you want to?"

"I hadn't even thought about it," he said,

"It seems only logical, now that you're sane again."

He gazed off, into the middle distance . . . "No, man."

"Wouldn't you like to sing with the band one more time?"

"Sure I would. But, I don't know if . . . "

"Come on, the whole world's waiting for it."

"No, Roy. I don't think so."

"Why not?"

"It would be hell on me, amigo. There would *really* be a million questions: 'Where have you been? How did you do it? Why did you do it? Why have you come back now? Tell us all about it . . . tell everything!' I'd be talking about my death-disappearance-resurrection for the rest of my life. It's all anyone would want to know. Everyone would want interviews and everyone would want to know the same thing."

"Hey, *I* want to know! I couldn't sleep when I got those letters. You sure have a way of driving people nuts."

"Yeah . . . I'm the one who makes you mad."

"You know, we could make some great music together. The drummer and the guitar player are still in shape, they play all the time. I play behind your poet buddy, Pat McClear. He reads, I play his words—just like *we* used to but without the drums and guitar. Man, *all* our chops are in great shape. Hell, you look like you're in great shape, except for . . . " I caught myself.

"Except for my cough, huh? Is that what you were going to say?"

"Well . . . yes."

"Don't worry. I'm fine."

"Then come back with me. Let's play! Don't worry about the interviews, we'll issue a press release—Denny Sullivan still works for us, for *you*—and we'll say you simply won't talk about it. Only the music. Only your words."

"I wouldn't even talk about my words. If I have to explain them . . . they're not working."

"Then what would you talk about?'

"What I do."

"And what exactly is that?"

He smiled, and I could see the peace in his eyes. "I live, my friend. I just live each day."

6

The sun moved heavily through its predetermined arc in the sky. The ceiling fans turned and slowly reshuffled the deck of steam enveloping the Bar Gauguin. Everything was lethargic in the afternoon heat. Everything seemed to be in slow motion. Including the Poet. He was no longer the exposed electrical wire of our youth. No longer the possessed shaman, the maniac, the wild child. He was a man now, he had found an inner peace. And I wanted to know how.

"Alright, man," I said. "If you don't want to go back, then why did your wife write to me? If you don't want to make music anymore . . ."

"Whoa, Roy," he interrupted. "I didn't say I don't want to make music. I love singing. And being on stage, standing in front of your wall of sound, you and the guitar player and the drummer, man, it was the best. The only place in the world I really belonged. But now, I belong to this island, this tiny little dot on the map. It's my home."

"And you're not going to risk the exposure."

"Exactly. I'm not going to risk losing this . . . among other things."

"What do you mean, 'other things'?"

The sun slipped through another degree of its arc. Two kids on bicycles rolled slowly past the front door, spokes strobing through the beaded curtain. The Poet watched the kids glide by, smiled, took a deep breath, and turned to me.

"Let me tell you the story. I know you're going to want to know everything, so I might as well start at the beginning."

I smiled, rolled my eyes. "Not from when we met in college. I know that story already."

"Yeah, we already lived it, didn't we?"

"Never had better times, amigo."

"Actually, neither did I. Except, of course, for today . . . and surely tomorrow."

"Your best day is coming tomorrow?"

He shook his head. "No, it's here now. And so is yours. Don't you think?"

I had to stop on that one. It sounded suspiciously Zen-like. I was confused, because toward the end of our band days he had reverted to type. He had become a Western man, living out a Greek myth of Dionysian inspiration and gargantuan proportion. His life was an over-indulgence of the senses, an intoxication of the flesh, a delirium. He had carried that infatuation to its extreme and he had become a satyr. Now he was famous for his satyriasis. He was worshipped as a demigod of the carnal. Back then he had mocked the faux-Indian, sitar, paisley-printed lifestyle of those young seekers of the 1960s. He even called the three of us—the guitarist, the drummer, and me—the East India Company because we had plunged ourselves into the study of ragas—much to the consternation of the Poet. That is, the Poet on alcohol and only in the company of his support team of reprobates, the La Brea Mafia.

"Don't tell me you're now a member of the East India Company?" I said jokingly.

"The what?"

"Remember calling your three musicians the 'East India Company' because we were into Ravi Shankar and Ali Akbar Khan?"

He thought, then shook his head. "Doesn't ring a bell. Was I drunk when I said it?"

"Whenever you were mean, you were drunk. Whenever you were an asshole . . . "

"Let me guess, I was drunk," he said sheepishly.

"And you were drunk too much of the time," I added.

"So I was a mean, sarcastic asshole most of the time?"

"A lot of the time."

"Christ, how did you put up with me?"

"Because I loved your poetry, man. The art came first. Above everything. And . . . well . . . I loved you."

An embarrassed silence descended from its hiding place just above the ceiling fans and settled awkwardly on our shoulders. The clock ticked unmercifully. Finally the Poet looked at me.

"Thanks, Roy. You were always there, weren't you?"

"Hell, we were all there for you. All three of us."

"Even the drummer?"

"Sure he was," I protested. "He loves you, too. But he's damned angry at you for drinking yourself to death."

"I guess he's got a right to be mad."

"I'll say, you old reprobate."

We both laughed, sipped our planter's punch and the embarrassment returned to its hiding place.

"Now, what I *really* want to know is about this Zen stuff. The best day . . . and tomorrow. You never talked like that back in Los Angeles."

"I didn't really *know* about any of that back in Los Angeles. I knew power, and abandon, and howling at the moon. I knew rage . . . oh, plenty of rage. Anger and rage are so easy for youth. Rage is a no-brainer. Any fool can do it. And the more I drank the more angry I became."

"At what?"

"At you!"

"Me? Why me?"

"And the drummer and the guitar player, too."

"But we were your foundation. We held you up."

"That's just it, I didn't want your support. I wanted to do it on my own. I didn't want to be held up by you three happy guys. You were so infuriatingly optimistic. So damned positive. It just made me . . . angry."

"At us? For what, for believing we could change the world?"

"Yeah, at you." And as he spoke the next words he had to look away from me. "Because you believed in the power of love. And I didn't."

The embarrassed silence came down again. But this time as a harpy, digging its claws into the backs of our necks. This one hurt.

"So you drank," I said at last.

He nodded. "And that's why I took up with those other three guys. They were the shadow of you. They represented you guys, but as losers. With them I could just drink the time away. Drink my life away. We'd get high, pick up chicks, play mind games with anybody we could get our nasty psychic teeth into, drive too fast, and too drunk . . . "

"Sounds like you were trying to kill yourself, amigo."

The harpy let go. Our frankness released her talons from our necks and she fluttered up to perch on the mahogany cross beams, blending into the darkness.

"You know, my friend, I *was* trying to kill myself. I didn't know what the fuck I was doing. I didn't know who I was, I didn't know *why* I was. I was a success, I was famous, I had money in the bank . . . and I had nothing. Except a bad hangover." He paused and stared at his drink. "And that's why I had to do it."

"Do what?"

"Stage my own death."

7

We were finishing our seventh record. It was our last legal obligation to the record company. Seven disks, seven chakras, seven steps to heaven."

"Seven and out," I said.

"Exactly. What better time to consider a life change? We were in the process of completing our contract. I would be a free man after the mixing of five more songs. And they were sounding great. I knew you guys could handle it without me. Hell, you usually did anyway. Singing the words was my part. All that technical, sixteen-track, E.Q., compressors, echo, reverb, slap-back, Neumann-47-mics, mix-down, A.K.G. shit, Roy, what does it all mean? And do I have to care?"

"Just make it sound good, huh?"

"And you always did," the Poet said. "You and the guitar player. I didn't have any worries about the sound. The words were great, the music was great, and the noise coming out of the speakers was great. All the plink, twang, rumble and boom were as they should be. All was right with the universe. Except me. I had to get away."

"You couldn't take it anymore?"

"I couldn't take *myself* anymore. And at the end of the mix of 'Angel Woman'—man, it was so good, like barreling down the San Diego freeway at dawn, heading for Tijuana . . . and sin—I knew I had to do it. It was time to split. So I went home, packed a bag, put Kimberly on a plane for Paris—she loved the idea—told her to see her junkie buddy, the Duke, have him rent us a furnished place—he got us digs in St. Germain within a week—told her to check in to the George V and I'd meet her there in a few days. I saw a couple of girls—for old times' sake, you know—drank too much with Tom, Mike, and Dog, didn't tell anybody anything, let the apartment go, and then I told you guys."

I remembered that day like it was yesterday. "I'm going to Paris tonight," he told us. "Why don't you guys just go ahead and finish off the record? You don't really need me for the mixes anyway." And then he tried a feeble joke, "Don't mix my voice too low, just 'cause I'm not here." It didn't get a laugh. It only drew a shocked silence. None of us could believe it. Paris? Tonight? How final it all sounded. How impetuous, but how terrifyingly final. A great, gaping fear spread through all of us: me, the drummer, the guitar player and the engineer. We had all been together since the first album, and now he was breaking the chain. The five of us looked at each other and I think our collective career flashed before our shared mind's eye in that moment of silence. Then the drummer spoke: "How long you going to be gone?" He knew. It was the only question that mattered: "How long?" We all knew *why* he was going. We could see it. He was a mess.

"I don't know," he answered. "A week, a month, six months. Maybe even a year . . . if I need it." And that "if I need it" was what broke my heart. He was telling us he knew what bad shape he was in and he was asking for our forgiveness, and our blessings. It occurred to me, at that instant, that this was his existential leap of faith. And I was proud of him. Continuing on his present course, he would have had maybe two years left. But instead, he was going to leap into the unknown. He was hoping to write again, I could feel it. He was going to be the *Poet* again. He was going to seduce the muse and be an artist again instead of a rock star.

"Paris, huh?" I said finally. "Well, I think it's a good idea, Jordan. Give you a chance to write."

And then the guitar player spoke: "Yeah, Paris. That's the place for you."

"An American in Paris," the engineer said. And the tension was broken. We had accepted his decision.

The Poet was greatly relieved. "I thought I'd compile all the notes I took at my trial in Texas. Maybe write a book on America and its obsessions."

I loved it. He was going to get down to work again. "I can't wait to read that," I blurted out in perhaps an overspirited *bonhomie*. "Your observations on the 'land of the free' while on trial for obscenity in Texas, the land of the gun."

"Yeah, do it!" the guitar player said. "And poems, too. Lots of poems."

Then the drummer spoke. "And songs, too, Jordan. Don't forget about your songwriting."

"Don't worry, man," he said. "I won't."

Then we all paused—there was nothing left to say. An angel passed over—the Angel Woman—and then we hugged him, each in our turn, and he said, "Well, I'll see ya." And he was gone.

I came back out of my memory flight. Back to the Bar Gauguin, in the city of Victoria, on the island of Mahé, in the Seychelles. I was with the Poet. And he was alive.

"So, old friend, did you ever write that book about America's obsessions?" I asked.

"No, Roy. I was more concerned with my own obsessions back then. But I did write a lot of poetry in Paris. I tried to do what I said I was going to do. I wrote. And I set up a schedule for myself, and I tried to stick to it. And you know what? . . . I did. In between bouts of drinking, that is. And the muse visited me once in a while. The writing was good. It had a flow to it. Euterpe came and sat with me, and caressed my thigh, and kissed my neck, and we made love on the little writing desk I had in that apartment in St. Germain."

"Which one is Euterpe?" I asked.

"The goddess of music and lyric poetry. She's our girl, the one who came into the studio with us and came to so many of our gigs. She's the one who worked the magic on us when we were a band. Then she came to me in Paris."

"Well, where *is* that poetry?" I was anxious to read it, excited by the possibilities.

"My ex-father-in-law has all of it," he answered.

I sighed with relief. "Thank God. I thought maybe you threw it away like you did those four notebooks of yours I found. They had a shitload of good writing in them, remember?"

"Roy, honestly I don't. Was it any good?"

"I just *said* it was." He could be so exasperating. "You left them behind at our place after you moved out. Dianna said she found them in a basket full of junk when we were packing to move. I leafed through them and there was all kinds of stuff—notes, songs, poems, jottings, aphorisms. Really good stuff. I thought you had misplaced them and were probably looking for them. So I rushed them to you—not before I had copied a few things down, however."

"Good thinking. Do you still have them?"

"You better believe I do."

"Why didn't you do anything with them?"

"I don't know. Seemed kind of sacrilegious."

The Poet laughed. "I'm not a religion, man."

"That's what you think. So anyway, about two months later I asked you if you had found anything we could use in them. And do you know what you said?"

He grinned. "You're going to tell me, aren't you. Regardless of what I say, you're going to take a small delight in telling me what an asshole I was, right?"

I laughed. "You're damn right I am. I don't know how many times I wanted to punch you out, but this was certainly one of them."

"You should have hit me," he said. "I'm sure I deserved it."

"That's what Dianna always said. She said you *wanted* to be hit. She thought you wanted that physical pain as a proof of love. That somehow you equated the two."

He winced at the ancient memory. "Ouch. That Dianna always had my number. She was right, you know—absentee, disciplinarian father, and all that. Man, she could see right through me. I always found it hard to look into her eyes. They were so dark and deep, like she could dig down into me with those eyes."

"That's what I love about her, that depth," I said. "She can see right through me, too. I love that. She's so honest . . . and so real."

"Hey, don't go on a rhapsody about your wife, now. You still have to hurt me a little about those four journals."

"That's right, I don't want to lose my anger."

"So, what did I say?"

I looked at him. "You said, 'I threw them away. It was just a bunch of early stuff . . . ' I wanted to strangle you."

"What can I say, man? Drunk again."

I punched him on the shoulder, mockingly. "Asshole!"

We sipped at our drinks. The fine and tropical and rum and fruit planter's punch.

"So how come your ex-father-in-law . . . what's his name?"

"Magellan. Magellan Manson."

"What the fuck kind of a name is that?"

"Obviously his parents were a little off the wall. Probably their one poetic act. They came from just below Bakersfield. The town of Weed Patch."

"Like the Okies in *Grapes of Wrath*?"

"Exactly the same place. They were Steinbeck Okies, but in real life."

"Well, see, that's literary," I said.

"Somehow, I don't think that's exactly how they saw it,"

"They named him Magellan, though."

"And he hated it.He called himself . . . get this . . . Bud!"

"How original," I smirked.

"Didn't one of our Presidents have a fucking dog named Bud?"

"Or Checkers."

"Or King Timahoe!" he said, laughing.

"Or Asta!"

"No, Roy. That's *The Thin Man* with William Powell and Myrna Loy."

"No, that's F.D.R." I said.

"Then they *both* had dogs named Asta."

"Which one came first?"

"Hell, I don't know. It's all before our time," he said.

"I know who would know . . . "

And we said it simultaneously. On the same wavelength again.

"Bud!"

We roared with laughter.

"Fucking *Bud*!" said the Poet.

And we roared again.

And it felt good to laugh with the Poet again, just like in the old days. And I made up my mind at that moment—I would bring him back with me, back into the band. The drummer and the guitar player would love to laugh with him again. They would love to bask in the new warmth of the Poet, so like the warmth of our beginnings on the beach in El Segundo, with his sense of humor, and his wit, and his profundity, and his laughter. Yes, I would take him back to the beach and he would write again. But now with a great peace and maturity. And a new-found wisdom.

"Jean-Luc," he called to the bartender. "*Conch frites, s'il vous plaît.*" To me he said, "I'm starved, aren't you?"

But before I could answer he clasped his arm around my shoulder and squeezed. "God, it's good to see you. I missed you. And the other guys, too. I missed laughing with you guys, and making music with you guys, and making plans and seeing them come to fruition. Man, we had fun, didn't we?"

I smiled at him and nodded. "Yes, I am hungry. And yes, we did have fun."

"We turned the whole thing on its head! I mean the whole damned thing! A transformation. A metamorphosis."

"And the whole country is dying to do it again," I said. "We're starved for an insight, for a new way of being. We've fallen back on a traditionalism, a fundamentalism. We need a new vision, and we're terrified of that vision. The whole country is on the horns of an existential dilemma and we need you! To *do* it. And that's why you're gonna go back with me. For the epiphany of a goddamned nation."

"Whoa, man, that's a tall order. Epiphany of a nation? I'm gonna have to mull that one over, amigo. Let it, you know, simmer awhile."

And then the food came. Deep fried strips of tenderized conch. Light and crispy and delicious. Like shrimp tempura or Italian calamari, but with its own distinctive seashell flavor. The Poet sprinkled salt and pepper on the golden, crinkly mound and we dug in, wolfing down those tender little strips of succulent shell animal.

"Good stuff, huh?" the Poet said through a mouthful. "The food on these islands is great." He swallowed his *conch frite*. "A Creole food, not unlike our own Cajun. It's a marriage of French and English by way of Africa." He laughed to himself. "Not unlike my *own* marriage."

"Can I meet your wife?" I asked.

"Of course. We'll have dinner tonight. She's a great cook. Takes great care of me, too. Me and the kids."

"You said you have two?"

"Yep. Boy and a girl."

"The perfect all-American family," I said.

"Hardly, man. We've mixed the races. The kids can't be put in a category. There's no longer any racial exclusiveness here. No more judging by skin color."

"Only the content of the heart, huh?"

"That's it. Is the heart open . . . or closed? Now eat your *frites*, they get soggy when they're cold."

And we dove back into the golden mound, stuffing our maws with French-fried goodness. The Poet held up a crisp strip, said "Ambrosia!", popped it into his mouth and grinned like a Cheshire cat. It was his trademark little-boy grin, sly and rebellious and seductive. The grin that made the girls fall madly in love with him during the years of our rock-stardom. It was both shy and revealing at the same time. It contained the implication that he would go all the way if you were willing to follow him. And thousands were, many thousands of nubile young things who were looking for a mythical lover were more than willing. And they continue to this very day to find an unrequited love in his image. Although he has been presumed dead for many years now, he still exerts that irresistible magnetic pull on women, a pull that registers in the loins and the dark places. He is their outlaw poet, eternal in death, perpetual in desirability. And that smile of his that contained all possibilities, including the possibility of death by extreme pleasure, took him into the arms of Thanatos, and we thought he was lost forever. His leather, his ringlets of hair—that lion's mane—the tilt of his head to one side as he pondered an answer to your question, the swelling of his neck as he sang—like some great, engorged and impossibly thick penis—the sinuous, seductive walk that would sway out from his hips like a reptile, and that smile . . . were gone. Gone forever. And we mourned him.

And yet here I was devouring *conch frites* with him and we were gabbing like the old days, the Poet and the keyboard player, and he was alive.

"Man, this conch is good," he said. "I've been devouring Jean-Luc's tapas for ten years now—maybe more, I don't know. It's hard to keep strict track of time here. And you know . . . it doesn't even matter. We live, and we die."

"I know, 'And not even death can end it.'"

"That's right. *A Prayer for the American Century.* I never got to compliment you. It's a great album. You guys did a brilliant job."

"Well, we had your words," I said, swelling with his approval. "They inspired us to give you your poetry album. The one you always wanted."

"Posthumously, of course," he said.

I laughed. "Not quite so posthumous as it seemed at the time, though." I punched him on the shoulder. " You goddamned *roué*, you're alive."

"Never felt this good in my *old* life, Roy." He reached for the last strip of conch and popped it into his mouth. "I needed that. Something to absorb the alcohol. Don't want to drink on an empty stomach, not at our age, anyway."

"Shall we have one more?" I asked.

"Oh, no. Two's my limit, man. I learned that a long time ago."

"Two a day? That's still a lot, these suckers are powerful."

"Come on . . . I mean two a week. Hey, do you think I'm still a drunk?"

"Well, you did set the mai tai record at the Kawai Village in Hawaii. Thirty mai tai's in one twenty-four hour period. Remember?"

"Obviously not! Did I really do thirty?"

"I counted."

"Jesus, what a maniac. I *should* be dead."

"Well, you're not! And we're gonna change the world, god-damn it. You're coming back and we'll continue on. We're gonna finally complete the great work."

"The alchemical 'Great Work,' huh?" he said. "The transformation from lead to gold."

"That's it," I said.

"But we can't do that for people, Roy. They have to change themselves. Each person has to make a leap of faith, and they have to make that leap alone. We can't be the messiah for them. In the new time, there won't even be a *need* for a messiah. No second coming. No *Mosiach*. No apocalypse. Just a gradual evolution of consciousness."

"We could help accelerate it, though. People will want to see you and hear what you have to say. Hell, *I* want to hear what you have to say."

"That's probably why Angelique sent for you, my friend. She wants you to hear my story."

"And I want the world to hear your story," I said. "There's been a change in you, man. You're a good and decent human being, now. You're not the Snake Man anymore."

He thought a bit. "Hell, who am I to tell anybody anything? An ex–rock star, who only wanted to be a poet, hiding out on some granite atoll in the middle of the Indian Ocean. What does it matter what I say? Who's listening, anyway?"

"Goddamn it, I'm listening. Why do you think I'm here? Why do you think I came all this way?"

"To bring 'em back alive," he laughed. "To capture a poet and bring him back to civilization. Like 'Kong the Magnificent!'"

His laughter was infectious. "Like Mighty Joe Young," I said. "The beast, subdued. Brought back from the wilds of Borneo to

Radio City Music Hall. Ladies and gentleman, for your amusement and edification!"

"Exactly!"

"Well, that's bullshit," I said. "You'll come back with me if you
want to, and we'll have a whole other mission than amusement.
It's called transformation!" I paused in my enthusiasm. "And
now I want to hear the story, okay? Enough throat clearing, pal,
let's hear it."

He sipped at the bottom of his planter's punch and made the
residual fruit juice gurgle, like a pre-pubescent sucking every last
bit of sweetness from the bottom of a 7-Eleven Slurpee. "Okay.
Here's what happened in Paris . . . "

"Wait a minute, what happened to the poetry you wrote in
Paris?"

"I told you," he said. "My ex-father-in-law has it."

"But I know nothing about it." I was confused. "Is it a secret
or something?"

The Poet shook his head. "No."

"Why hasn't he shown it to me? Or just published it himself?
Or done *anything* with it?"

"I have no idea," the Poet said. "He's just sitting on the stuff.
Not that I really care, anymore. But why is he hoarding it? I
didn't write it for him. It's for the people, our fans."

"And he has control of your poems, the legal rights?"

"That's what I've heard," he said. "Evidently my father didn't
want anything to do with his 'degenerate son's' literary output,
so the rights went to Kimberly's father after she died."

"How do you know all this?" I asked.

"Marie-Therese kept me informed of the legal machinations
concerning the hundred and fifty pounds of bricks buried in that
cemetery in Paris." He chuckled to himself.

"So she was in on it!"

"And so was her boyfriend, Claude," he said.

I shook my head in amazement. "And they never said a word to anyone?"

"Hell, no. I swore them to secrecy with an oath! They're French, they love that kind of conspiracy shit. *Trés romantique.*"

"A hundred and fifty pounds of bricks."

"Yep, buried in Paris as yours truly," he said. "Of course we had to put sand in there, too. Keep the bricks from rattling around."

"You son of a bitch," I said. "So the rumors are true. One hundred and fifty pounds of sand . . .

"Pretty much true."

"A sealed coffin?"

"Correct," he nodded. "Had to be, of course. Couldn't have people throwing themselves on the mortal remains of the Snake Man—with weeping and beating of breast and rending of flesh. The Snake Man wasn't there."

"And the death certificate, signed by an Algerian doctor? It said your heart stopped."

"Correct, but it wasn't an Algerian."

"What, then?"

"A Moroccan."

I laughed, "There's a difference? And five thousand dollars American. As a payoff."

The Poet shook his head. "Now that's where the rumors are wrong."

"There was no payoff?"

"Are you kidding? Try *ten* thousand American."

"I don't care about the amount . . . "

"Well, I did," he said. "I had to pay it."

"I'm more interested in the truth of the rumors."

"They're true."

"But, how do they know?" I asked. "I mean, how did they even get started?"

He thought a bit. "You've heard of people spreading false rumors?"

"Of course."

"Well . . . these are true rumors." He smiled. "And we'll never know how they got started."

"It's almost as if people divined the truth out of the air of Paris," I said.

We both smiled, and the ceiling fans stirred the steam. The bartender cleaned our empty plates and our empty glasses. The Poet ordered water. "*Deux bouteilles de l'eau, s'il vous plait.*"

"*Gazeux?*" the bartender queried.

The Poet nodded, and two bottles of Perrier appeared, all moist and beaded and frosted. The bartender produced two small glasses and we set to it, washing down the sweet drink and the crackly fry.

"But what about Kimberly?" I asked. "How come she didn't know?"

"She wasn't there," he said. "She had gone off with the Duke to Corsica."

I was incredulous. Kimberly was his soul mate, his incendiary lover who finally had him to herself in Paris. "She left you for the Duke?"

"No, no. Nothing like that. I sent her with him."

"To Corsica . . . why?"

"For the powder. The white powder."

"Ohh . . ."

"China white. *La Chinoise blanche,* as they called it in Paris.

She didn't object. He was on a buy, Corsican Mafia or something equally illegal and debased. Romantic, as Kimberly saw it."

"She could have been busted," I protested.

"The Duke was very well connected. Hell . . . he was a duke. And besides, she had to be out of town for my death. I told her to take her time, enjoy the scenery."

"See Napoleon's birthplace, I suppose."

"That's exactly what I told her to do," he smiled. "How'd you know?"

"Because you're a sarcastic smart-ass. At least you were."

"Angelique tells me I still am."

"Then she's a good woman," I said. "She can tell you the truth about yourself. We never could."

"Nobody could have, back then." He smiled wickedly. "But we've established that, haven't we?"

I paused, thinking. The Seychelles were heavenly. And he was happy here. I wondered if I actually should take him back? But we needed him. He was a breath of fresh air from the middle of the Indian Ocean.

"So what happened with Kimberly . . . and your death?" I said, falling back into the story.

"Well, we did the deed while she was away. Got the coffin, filled it with the requisite bricks and sand, sealed it with nails and screws. Sealing it was the key part."

"And that's the damned part that has given rise to all the rumors of you being alive," I said. "All the sightings, the books, the speculations . . . that fucking sealed coffin. Brilliant. Who thought of it?"

"Marie-Therese," he said. "The women are ultimately so much more inventive than we are. She knew there would be hysteria from Kimberly and my secretary. She said, 'Seal the coffin!' Just like that. And Claude and I both said what you just said . . . 'brilliant.' The logic, the *emotional* logic was simply inspired. So we did it, and then it was time for *le docteur*. Claude went into one of the darker areas of town, the Marais, and concluded the arcane negotiations he had begun two weeks earlier when we conceived the plan."

"So they were in on it from the beginning."

"Oh, yes," he said. "I couldn't have done it without them. Hell, they picked the cemetery, too."

"Nice touch . . . all those artists. With the trees and the cobblestones, the stray cats and the ornately carved markers. It's charming."

"Yeah, maybe too charming," he said. "I just wanted them to dump the coffin in some plain cemetery, virtually an unmarked grave. But they both said no. They felt that the dead American rock star should receive a poet's resting place. He should be interred with his peers. Something nice, something proper. They knew there would be pilgrimages. They knew the young people of Paris . . . and, well, I guess all of Europe would find it . . . "

"Now it's the world, my friend."

The Poet nodded. "And they find it irresistible, don't they?"

"Marie-Therese and Claude were right," I said. "That gravesite has become a secular shrine."

He said, "And that's why it had to be in that charming artists' graveyard. If the young rock-and-rollers had started trekking to some workingman's graveyard, it wouldn't have made sense."

I understood. "People would have asked questions. 'Why is the famous, rich, American rock star buried in such mundane surroundings?'"

"Exactly," the Poet said.

"And then they would have begun to wonder if you were actually under the ground."

"Exactly."

"And then they would have suspected a hoax . . . "

"Right again."

"And perhaps demanded an exhumation."

"Those were Claude's very words."

"So they arranged for the *charming* resting place."

"But they couldn't do it before Claude had the death certificate. No funeral arrangements could be made until I was legally dead."

I jumped in, unable to control my excitement at the unraveling of the mystery. "And Claude went to the Moroccan doctor with the money. The ten thousand dollars."

"Ten thousand dollars, *American,* as they say in Paris. You know, the real moola. The greenbacks!" He smiled to himself, probably reliving the adeptness of the plan and its execution.

"Hey, don't stall out now," I said. "What happened next?"

He continued to smile, remembering. "Then we had to move fast."

8

I had a plane ticket to the Seychelles," the Poet said. "It was leaving that night—July 2nd. I was going to do it on July 4th, but I thought that might be a bit obvious."

"But a plane ticket in your own name?"

"No, Roy. In the name of one, you'll love this, Joseph Phoenix."

"Like the city in Arizona?"

"Yes . . . but more the mythological—reborn out of the flames and ashes. The bird-man, risen."

"But I thought you were the *word*-man."

"I was," he said. "But this was the new adventure. The beginning of a new life. And I was free!"

I had to laugh. "As Joseph Phoenix? Who the hell would believe 'Joseph Phoenix'?"

"Everybody. It was right there on the passport. Who's going to question an American passport? Especially the places I went."

"But listen . . ."

"Nobody really cares about passports outside of the good old U.S. of A. And some of northern Europe."

"Wait a minute . . ."

"The small countries, the poor countries, they don't give a shit. You want to come in? Come in. As long as you're not carrying drugs. It's a piece of cake."

"Hold it already, man. How did you get a phony American passport?"

"In Paris? Not really that hard. French Algerians, or maybe it was French-connection Marseilles Mafia types, I really don't know. Claude and Marie-Therese took care of it. I just took a couple of photos . . ."

"Christ, how much did it cost?"

"Less than the death certificate. Five thousand, American. Seems the phony passport business is a lot more competitive than the phony death certificate game."

"Not a lot of people staging their own deaths, huh?"

He laughed. "Not your everyday scam."

"How long did it take to get a forged American passport?" I asked.

"One week."

"Jesus Christ, how simple."

"Oh, yeah? You try it, man."

I smiled. "Maybe next lifetime. When I come back as the lead singer."

That tickled him. "Forget it, amigo. Lead singer ain't worth it, ask the man who was one."

"Okay, back to the plan," I said. "What next?"

"I picked up a bag with new clothes at Claude's—I had to leave all my old clothes at our apartment."

"Of course. 'If he's dead, why are his clothes missing?'"

The Poet nodded. "We had to cover all the bases, right?"

"You didn't even take your leather pants?"

"Hell, no. Damn things didn't fit anymore, anyway."

"Well, what happened to them?"

"I have no idea."

"There's a rumor floating around that one of Kimberly's junkie friends sold them for some China White."

"Sounds about right. You should have seen those sleazeballs. Decadent Euro-trash aristocrats, sell a guy's fucking *pants* for junk. She sure could pick 'em."

"In the end, I guess they killed her. Didn't they?"

A sadness entered his eyes. "She was a good girl. She just got mixed up with the wrong crowd." He swallowed and turned his head. "In a way, back then, as much as I could . . . I loved her."

I put my hand on his forearm. "I know you did, man. You were good to her."

"No I wasn't. I was a shit to her." His eyes grew moist and his voice was thick with emotion. "I didn't want her to die," he said. "I never intended for that to happen. I just wanted to get away. I *had* to get away, or *I* would have died."

I squeezed his arm in empathy. "She probably wouldn't have lasted much longer than she did, running with that junkie set. It's not your fault. Hell, didn't the Duke OD?"

"That's what I heard," he said, wiping at his eyes. He cleared his throat, took a sip of Perrier . . . and then the cough hit him again. A bad cough.

"Christ, man, that cough sounds awful. What's wrong?"

He took a few swallows and regained his composure. "Nothing, really. Doctor said to quit smoking, that's all."

"Well, have you?"

"At least three years ago. Just an occasional cigar, though. We get them from Cuba here. A Cohiba and a five star brandy? Man, can't give that up now, can I?"

He seemed better. The cough had abated. "Too many of those black French cigarettes, huh?"

"Those damned *Gauloises* and *Bleu Caporals*. Sure were good with a café au lait, though. But that's all over now."

I was reassured. "Good! But did you give up coffee, too?"

"Naw, my gut likes it. I can eat or drink anything. It's my lungs I have to watch out for. Bit of a congenital disorder. Runs in the family on my mother's side. No big deal. I've got it under control."

"Good!" I said again. "You've got to take care of yourself. We've got a lot of work ahead of us."

"So you say."

He didn't sound overly enthusiastic about the prospects.

"Well, it won't really be work," I said. "It'll be fun!"

"I know, Roy. Making music was always fun. But I'm just a little tired, now. I've got to get this cough under control."

"You will, man. What did the doctor say it was?"

"Tars and nicotines. Just got to let it dissipate, that's all. They say it takes seven years to replace every cell in your body. My lungs only have four to go."

"Good! And don't inhale those cigars, either."

"Man, you don't inhale a Cohiba. "You just get the globe of it in your mouth. You hold it there, tasting it, and then you exhale. And then a little taste of brandy . . . "

"So don't even get the globe of it. As a matter of fact, don't even smoke cigars at all. Don't smoke anything." I was being his older brother again.

"Not even pot? No marijuana?"

"Definitely not marijuana. Too many goddamned tars. Hell, I had a smoker's cough from the residue of that stuff. I used to cough my fool head off back in El Segundo. And we were just kids."

"I haven't smoked any grass in ages," he said. "Had some nice hash in India about . . . ohh . . . twenty years ago. But that was it. That was the last time before I went up into the mountains."

"I haven't smoked anything in years, either." And then his last sentence registered. "Mountains?" I said. "What mountains?"

"That's a big jump in the story, Roy. We just got me a ticket to the Seychelles and a passport for Joseph Phoenix. Don't you want to hear the progression?"

"Of course. But don't just curve-ball words like 'India' and 'into the mountains' at me. I can barely handle *sitting* here with you."

"All right, I'll try to be orderly. But first a brandy. I think we both could use one." He called to the bartender: "Jean-Luc, *deux cognac. Remy Martin, s'il vous plait.*"

"*Oui, Monsieur Phoenix,*" came the reply.

"So you've kept the name Joseph Phoenix ever since you, well . . . died."

"That's me. Middle name Kyle."

"I get it," I laughed. "One Joseph K.?"

"Exactly. One for my man Kafka."

"For the absurdity of it."

"Yep. And Phoenix for the . . . well, for the transcendence of it."

I regarded him closely. "You didn't use that word back then."

He smiled. "I do now."

The cognac arrived in cut-glass snifters.

"I know what the word means, now," he said.

"Well, continue with the disappearing act of Joseph K. But I must tell you, I'm really intrigued by the idea of the transcendence."

"I'll get to it." He sniffed his cognac. He seemed to be rolling the aroma around in his glass. It looked as if he was calling forth the essence, the secret of the liquid, and then inhaling that essence. A minor act of alchemy, but an impressive act of immersion in the moment. Like a man aware of the infinity of choices and yet totally absorbed—at home in the immediate.

He sipped the cognac, held it in his mouth, closed his eyes and swallowed. His corded neck muscles propelled the liquid down his throat as his Adam's apple bobbed in place. I'd seen that neck in action before, when he was singing in the recording studio. And that neck would swell, and ripple, and contort itself; transform itself into a constrictor snake wrapping itself around its own poetic phrases.

He opened his eyes and continued: "So there we stood, the three of us, for the last time in that apartment in St. Germain. Claude had the death certificate. Marie-Therese had had the coffin delivered to the apartment the day before. She said it was for an 'art piece.' We weighted it down and sealed it. I had my new passport, my new suitcase, my new clothes, my new name, and my plane ticket. Air Afrique, one way—Dar es Salaam to the Seychelles."

"But you needed money," I said. "You never wrote our accountant for money."

"Oh yes I did. You just didn't know about it. He wired me a hundred thousand dollars. I opened a Swiss bank account.

He never knew what I did with the money, and he was too cool to ask."

"He once told me, after you died, that he thought the hundred thou was for Kimberly's dope. That's why he never mentioned it."

"Nope. That was my 'traveling' money. And it lasted me a *long* time."

"You were overdrawn on our band account by about two hundred and fifty K . . . mister Joseph K."

"A hundred for that stupid clothing store of hers. 'Artemis.' Another fifty we spent in Paris. And my hundred K 'death tax.' Yeah, about two fifty. That was a lot of money for the early '70s."

"No kidding. So how the hell did you manage to spend all of your money and then go into the red, to us, to the tune of 250 thousand dollars?"

He looked slightly embarrassed. "Riotous living, my friend. I paid for everything, and everybody."

"Including Tom, Mike, and Dog. And that bottomless money pit movie you were making with them . . . 'The Open Road.' Jesus . . . can I tell you now?"

"I see it coming," he said. "Should I duck?"

"That movie *sucked,* man."

"I thought it was good at the time."

"Too much drugs and booze, amigo. Clouded your judgement."

He nodded thoughtfully, "Probably so. You know, I should never have had a credit card."

I laughed. "No shit, but I imagine you didn't have one when you left Paris, did you?"

"Nope. It's been strictly cash ever since. Occasionally I write a check on the Swiss account, but rarely."

"How could a hundred K last all this time?" I asked. "You must have done something for money!"

"Marie-Therese sent me a share of the profits from her movie. I helped her write it, or rather, rewrite it."

"*Angel Woman,* I remember it. She used our song. I talked to her on the phone. She gave me a sob story, never mentioned anything about your being alive and got me to give her a sync license for seven hundred and fifty dollars. Peanuts, my friend. We were being offered fifty K for that song at the time and I let her have it for seven hundred and fifty dollars. Chicken feed. Just because we owed it to you, as a kind of a tribute. And because she had gotten you into the *artistes'* cemetery. Goddamn, if I had known . . . "

"What would you have done?"

I paused for a beat, and smiled. "Hell, I'd have given it to her for seven hundred and fifty dollars anyway."

He laughed. "Well, there you are. That little largesse of yours made it possible for the movie to go into profit . . . and that made it possible for her to send me some bucks to keep me going."

"How long did that last?"

"Until I learned how to do it on my own."

"Doing what?"

"Nothing much," he said. "Writing articles for the local paper. Buying and selling trinkets. Little baubles. Asian art."

"You're an art dealer *and* a writer, now?"

"I'm whatever I have to be to stay alive . . . and keep my family alive."

I had to pause on that one. He had become a man of responsibility, and it was good to see. But how had it come about? Had something happened to him in those mountains? I sipped my cognac as various scenarios flashed through my mind. He put his snifter to his lips, and let the warmth flow into his body— obviously a practiced move. He hadn't quit drinking, but he seemed to have it under control. And as I looked at him, I realized he had *everything* under control.

"So I went to Orly, the Paris airport, and was gone. Simple as that. The hard part was back at that apartment after I left."

"What was the hard part?" I asked.

"The police!" he said. "*Les flics*. They had to be notified. After all, a dead body was found in an apartment in St. Germain, in the city of Paris."

"But why? They had a death certificate. Everyone knows the story of that death certificate and its vagueness. It said your heart stopped—complications resulting from a congenital lung problem, or words to that effect."

"Exactly. But the doctor had to call the police. An official notification, you understand."

I continued. "So the flics arrive, the doctor has left after his call, your friends are there—the women weeping, I suppose—the man hands the cops the death certificate, they read it, everything is in order, they see the coffin in the living room . . . it was in the living room, wasn't it?"

"That's where it was."

"Didn't they demand to see the body? Seeing a coffin in an apartment, didn't they want it opened?"

"Sure, but this is how the Fates work," he said, "if they're on your side. Claude wrote me later and told me the whole story. Make a hell of a movie, too. You know, you could do it, Roy. But you couldn't use real names . . . you'd have to fictionalize the characters, of course." He smiled to himself, liking the idea. "Or maybe a novel. Yeah . . . why not? You're always looking for a good story to tell, this could be it."

"How do you know I'm always looking for . . ."

"I keep tabs on you, man. And besides, I *know* you—you big windbag."

I laughed. "Forget about me, get on with your story. So what about the Fates?"

"Okay . . . so the cops see the coffin," he continued, "and they want to see the body. One of them—there were two—tries to open it. It's sealed. He says 'Open zis!' Claude and Marie-Therese play dumb through their tears. 'How can we, it's sealed,' Claude says. 'With a hammer or a crowbar,' says the cop. 'I don't have one,' says Claude. 'Well, find one!' says the cop. And he begins to search the apartment for a fucking crowbar. They're all digging through everything—and there's no hammer, no crowbar, nothing.

A knife! The cop finds a nice big *Sabatier* blade in the kitchen. 'Zis might work!' And he sticks the blade between the lid and the body of the coffin and begins to try to pry them apart. Claude said he was getting worried; there seemed to be a little movement. The flic wedged the knife here and there, cursing under his breath. The lid was starting to give ever so slightly. Claude said he was beginning to sweat. *Would they find the sand and bricks? Would the whole plan blow up?* Marie-Therese was about to panic. The flic was now pushing hard—it was working. And at that instant . . . Bam! The door flies open! And in rushes Kimberly! With bags and weeping and screaming and the Duke and my secretary and all manner of hysteria. And bam, the knife blade breaks! Perfect synchronicity. Door flies open, Kimberly screams, knife blade breaks! The room is now in a state of pandemonium. The cops have lost control. The wedged blade has broken off at the handle and women are weeping. Kimberly throws herself on the coffin, hysterical. One of the cops tries to go to her, to console her . . . and trips over her dropped baggage. He falls to the floor, kicking a bag open, spilling underwear, bras, and cosmetics. The other cop says 'Idiot' and begins to help his partner to his feet. As he's doing so he's stepping all over Kimberly's silk panties. My secretary dives on the floor to retrieve the unmentionables and save them from the jack-booted thug's crushing heels."

I had to stop him. "They weren't wearing jack-boots, were they? Like L.A. cops?"

"Poetic license, Roy. Allow me to embellish the story, will you?"

"Okay, okay. So continue."

"So . . . there's big-time chaos, with people crawling on the floor, a fallen flic, an hysterical woman, the sarcophagus of the Snake Man, a jack-booted thug, the broken blade, Claude and Marie-Therese milling about making faux-moaning and com-miseration sounds . . . "

"And the Duke?" I asked.

"Split, man. Out the door. Les flics and a coffin? He's out of there. Claude said the Duke very unobtrusively, very quietly sucked in his vibrations, turned around, and walked out. And they never saw him again. Of course Kimberly did—and far too many times for her own good."

He looked off, dreamily. He swirled his cognac and sniffed at it. He seemed to withdraw for a moment, almost as if he was seeing Kimberly's ghost pass before his eyes. He took a sip of his very good French brandy, let the warmth of it chase away the specter, and continued.

"So the cops had had enough. This was just too much hysteria. It wasn't worth the humiliation. Besides, their asses were covered. They had a death certificate. There was no foul play, nothing to investigate. They gave their condolences to Kimberly after Marie-Therese explained to them who she was—the deceased's betrothed—and they were gone! The Fates had saved the day."

"What amazing timing," I said.

"Well, the *Moirai* weren't going to let me get caught before my journey even began. Clotho had her own web spun for me, and evidently it didn't include the French flics."

"Who are the Moirai?"

"The Fates, the three sisters."

"Greek?"

"Yeah. Clotho, the spinner of the thread of life. Lachesis, who measures the thread. And Atropos . . . who cuts the thread."

"Oh, man, more spooky stuff," I said. "But in a way, the spinner is kind of like, uhh . . . "

"Like the Hindu web of *Maya*. Same impulses, more or less, but different cultures. That's what's so fascinating about being alive. The impulses of man are the same all over the world. We're all human, with the same needs and desires . . . but we tell the stories in a thousand different ways. The same archetypes wearing a thousand different cloaks."

"The same patterns, endlessly repeated in an endless variety of forms," I said.

He grinned and wagged a finger at me. "You've been reading your Joseph Campbell, haven't you?"

"Sure have. And you?"

"Read 'em all . . . more or less. Even through the alcohol I was always able to read."

"When did you finally stop drinking?" I asked.

He paused for a bit, looked at his snifter, and took a discrete sip. "When I'd had enough," he said.

"Simple as that?"

"That's the secret. An addict will stop—and I was definitely addicted to booze—when he's had enough."

"And that happened here in Victoria?"

"Yep . . . right here in the Seychelles. One morning I woke up and said to myself: 'If I keep doing this, I'm going to die.'"

"I had that same realization onstage at the Irish Mist," I said.

"That was the first club we played on the Sunset Strip. God, that was fun."

"I'm surprised you remember," I said sarcastically.

"Hey, man, I remember everything, except for the blackouts, of course. I haven't lost my mind here, you know. I finally found it." He paused and gave me a searching look.

"So tell me about your realization of death. Onstage, and at the Irish Mist to boot."

"We had been drinking. You and me. I was fucking drunk. Hell, so were you. We staggered on stage—remember that tiny little stage?—and began a set on an empty, like, Tuesday or Thursday night. We were giggling and carrying on and generally being assholes."

"So what? No one in the club, right?"

"Hell, never was. We were in the middle of some improvisation . . . on some song about death, or loss, or madness . . . and I'm boozily searching for the muse, and you come up to me, reach into your pocket, pull out an ampule of amyl-fucking-nitrate, and crack it under my nose. I inhale a deep blast, you inhale a deep blast, you put it back under my nose, I inhale again . . . and fall off my fucking stool! The drummer and guitar player keep playing, you're laughing like a fucking satyr—I can hear all this off in the distance, like deep in an echo chamber or a tunnel, and I begin to drift out of my body. Lying on the stage, at the Irish Mist on the Sunset Strip, at our first real club gig, I'm drifting out of my body. I'm fucking *dying*! I'm going off-planet, into the ether. I'm gone. And then the drummer, God bless him, crashes a cymbal! He whacks his Zildjian as hard as he can, and that nerve-shattering metallic shriek calls me back to Earth. All my nerve endings shiver, my body twitches with a few spasms, and

I'm back. You're still laughing and leering with maniac eyes and I get off the floor, sit on my stool, get back to playing my organ—my Slavic-ice solo of death—and everything is okay again."

"And that's when you said to yourself: 'If I keep doing this shit . . . I'm gonna die'?"

"Yeah, and I was terrified."

"Well you're a lucky man. It took me about seven more years, a blown career, no money in the bank, and a serious liver problem to come to that realization."

I smiled. "Yeah, but you're still here, you son of a bitch."

He smiled back. "Yeah, I sure am," he said, and raised his glass for a toast. "*L'Chaim* . . . .To life!"

"To life," I said.

We clinked our cut-glass snifters. They pealed out a tiny, sweet, bell tone, and we sipped our fine French cognac. It was good to be alive. And it was good to be with the Poet. Again.

"Come on. I need to stretch my legs," the Poet said. "Let's go over to the park. There's a big old banyan tree with benches underneath its limbs. Plenty of shade. Great for sitting and talking." He rose slowly from the barstool, and then grabbed the bar rail for support. "Whoa . . . I feel a little lightheaded. I've surpassed my weekly limit in one day. Must be gettin' old, huh?"

"Just mellow, my friend. Mellow and cooler and wiser," I said as I rose from my stool. And then it hit me, hard behind the knees. My body began to sway and I quickly reached for the rail. "Whoa, I see what you mean . . . can't hold it anymore."

"You just stood up too quickly."

"But you didn't," I said. "And it hit you, too."

"Well, I'm not in the best of shape. I've got to start working out. Maybe pump some iron. Maybe I'll start swimming again."

My head began to clear. "That's what I want to hear," I said. "I want you hard and lean and mean one more time. We got a lot of work to do when we get back, good work."

"I may be able to get hard and lean, but I'll tell you, Roy . . . I'll never be mean again."

He threw a wad of money on the bar. I picked it up and stuffed it in his shirt pocket. "No way, man. I pay. I'm the rich rock star, not you!"

He laughed. "Well, give Jean-Luc a nice tip, too. He always takes good care of me." He called out to the bartender, "Don't you, *mon ami*?"

"*Oui*, Monsieur Phoenix. It is my pleasure. *Je vous en prie*," said Jean-Luc from his end of the bar. He had taken up a position at a discreet distance from us, but not far enough away to miss a word of the conversation. He now felt a need to speak his heart. "Please, Monsieur Phoenix, do not go back to America."

The Poet looked at him, puzzled. "Why not, *mon ami*?"

"I fear for you," he said. There was a slight panic in the bartender's eye, as if he had seen something, something dark and beyond words.

"Thank you for your concern, Jean-Luc. But I will be fine. There is nothing to fear."

I put a handful of multi-colored bills on the bar and we stepped tentatively out into the bright, subtropical light. I immediately reached for my sunglasses. The Poet only squinted slightly.

"Don't you need shades?" I asked.

"Acclimation, Roy. And besides, I'm not a night person anymore. I can take the light. I've got nothing to hide."

9

The noonday heat had begun to subside. We walked on in a slightly boozy silence, past the shops and colorfully dressed locals and absurdly dressed tourists.

The Poet pointed to a holiday couple in matching lime and fuschia, paisley patterned resort wear, complete with protruding milky white limbs. "The English," he said.

"How do you know?" I asked.

"No one else on earth would have the bad taste to walk around in outfits like that. My blood kin, on holiday. And to think they once ruled the world."

"So did the dinosaurs."

"Ah, how the mighty have fallen," he said.

We turned a corner, and there it was. The enormous banyan tree. A Bengali ficus. It seemed to shade an area of fifty yards, maybe more. It was easily ninety feet high and its trunk would require at least ten men holding hands in a circle to gird its circumference. It sent out its great limbs like an umbrella, offering shade and respite to any and all creatures that needed it. Benches were scattered about in its dappled light. Mothers watched their children playing. Men read the daily paper. Lovers basked in the glow of their newly found common energy. Old men merely watched the parade of life in that wonderful square, in the city of Victoria, on the island of Mahé, in the Seychelle islands, somewhere due east of Mombassa, in the middle of the Indian Ocean.

"What an incredible tree," I said.

"It's ancient," said the Poet. "No one really knows how old it is . . . but they say the Buddha planted it."

"Did he come to these islands?"

"Who knows? After his enlightenment he traveled everywhere, teaching the four noble truths. Perhaps he came here, saw the need for comforting shade—a place he could speak from—and planted our tree."

"And now *we're* going to sit in its shade and plan our future."

"Maybe, Roy. But let's grab a bench before they're all gone. This is a popular spot when the heat finally breaks."

"I can see why. It's so . . . peaceful."

"Ain't it," he smiled. "That's why I'm here."

" And you've got to tell me how you got here."

We took a bench under the great spread of limbs, stretched luxuriously, filled our lungs with the sweet air of the tropics and he continued. "Let's see, where was I in this mad-brain tale of tightrope walking?"

"The Fates had just kept the coffin sealed," I said.

"Ah, yes. The Moirai. The three Greek sisters had created chaos and the flics had split."

"And the Duke had slipped out," I added. "And Kimberly was weeping."

"Hysterically, or she would have had the presence of mind to open the coffin herself. Instead, she went into the bathroom, no doubt shot up some of the good new Corsican smack, came out ten minutes later—according to Claude—flopped down in a chair and just sobbed softly to herself, repeating 'He's gone, he's gone, he's gone!' over and over."

As the Poet spoke, his eyes began to well up with tears.

"I loved her, Roy. I didn't want to hurt her . . . but I had to."

I put my arm around his shoulder, "You would have died . . . or gone mad if you had stayed. Besides, she had the Duke. It wasn't as if you left her all alone. And you left her your money in your will, didn't you?"

He wiped his eyes with a fist. "She got everything. I tried to take care of her financially."

"And you did," I said. "You didn't know she would OD. That wasn't your fault. That was the Duke."

"His fucking heroin killed her . . . and then it turned around and bit *him*. Serves him right, fucking Euro-trash. Talk about a case of bad karma." He shook his head as though trying to rid it of an evil memory.

"Anyway," he continued, "when I left Paris that day, riding on a plane to the Seychelles, I was Joseph Phoenix. I was drunk out of my mind and I was a mad man. Claude and Marie-Therese had the sealed coffin containing the mortal remains of me, the Snake Man, lowered into the ground. An early morning cere- mony, in that artists' graveyard, complete with weeping mistress, secretary . . . "

"And manager. Don't forget Phil Simmons. He was there, too. I must say, he handled it all—especially the press—very nicely. Except for the sealed coffin part. He really blew that."

"He was just a kid," the Poet said. "Give him a break. He did fine. No one could have handled the sealed coffin part. Especially Phil."

"Why do you say that?"

"Because, and you probably don't know this or you wouldn't have been so hard on him, his father was buried in a sealed coffin."

"His father?

"And if he had opened that coffin, my coffin, he might just have seen . . . his father."

"No wonder he didn't demand to see the body—I mean your body," I said. "Psychic transference. One authority figure for another. His father, his employer. Shit, he worshipped you. And probably really missed his father."

"Yeah, so lighten up on him, Roy."

"I really owe him an apology. I've been ragging on him ever since he came back from Paris."

"Maybe we can hire him again." He looked over at me, smiled his Cheshire cat grin, and winked. "When we get back to the States."

I couldn't believe it. Just like that he said "get back to the States." He had changed his mind! He was going to do it—it was more than a pipe dream, he was into. He was even thinking of a manager. "No, I want to hire the kid who was our office boy, Denny Sullivan. He's a man now and very competent, very sharp."

"That's fine with me," the Poet said. "As long as we don't hype our 'reunion' into some kind of crusade. I want everything to be low key." He gave me the Cheshire cat again. "You know, tasteful, befitting men of our . . . maturity."

I laughed with delight. "No smoke machines, huh? You probably don't want any elephants, either."

He laughed. "No circus, Roy. Just music."

"Funny, that's the way I see it, too."

"Maybe that's one of the reasons we were together, huh? Now what about Denny? Can he handle the gig?"

"Absolutely," I said. "And he loves you."

"I hear Kimberly liked him, too."

I laughed. "Hell, they shot up together."

"Is he clean now?"

"Of course. But he's always fighting the temptation. The monkey sits on his back, just waiting for an opportunity to squeal in his ear, waiting to be fed, always hungry. And Denny has to beat the damned thing with a stick to make it shut up."

The Poet spoke thoughtfully: "Don't I know that feeling. The alcohol worm that lives in my throat would always like a taste, too. He slithers up from deep in my gut to the back of my tongue when there's any anxiety. I've got him under control, now. But he's definitely a cousin of the junk monkey. Always there, always thirsty."

"Well, Denny's handling it fine. And so are you, my friend. You look better than I've seen you . . . "

"In the last couple of decades," he said, laughing.

I smiled at that one, and we sat back on the bench. The tropic air caressed us, and it was good to be alive. It was good to be with the Poet again—planning our future, one more time. After a moment of peace, he continued his story:

"So that was it. The coffin was buried and I was dead. Phil Simmons took care of the press releases, no doubt called you and the other guys . . . "

"After it was in the ground, of course."

"I've always wondered: Why was he there in the first place? Claude didn't call him."

"Kimberly called him. Said something about 'He's dead' over and over into the phone, and then just hung up the receiver. Simmons called me, I thought it was jive, but I told him to get his ass over to Paris, anyway. He was ahead of me, though. He already had a ticket booked on the noon flight."

"So Kimberly *tried* to be responsible. She called our manager."

"Yeah, and he went to Paris, walked into the apartment, saw the sealed coffin . . . and freaked. Now, I heard this part of the story third-hand, but evidently he told his buddy, Evan, that he was really stressed out, collapsed in a big reading chair—your chair, I assume—saw a little pile of white powder on an end table next to the chair, rolled a bill into a tube, and snorted a couple of hastily drawn lines, assuming it was cocaine. Twenty minutes later he was puking his guts out in the bathroom, and stayed weird and woozy for the next three days."

"Jesus Christ, it wasn't cocaine, it was Kimberly's China white!" the Poet exclaimed. "The poor kid. He never knew what hit him."

"He finally called me from Paris, and said you were not only dead . . . you were buried, too."

"What did you think?"

"Honestly? I said to myself, 'See, asshole! See what you get for drinking so much! Now you're fucking dead! You fucking asshole. Serves you right.' And then I broke down and cried." And *my* eyes began to well up with tears. It was his turn to put his arm around me. His strong hand clutched my shoulder for support as he said: "God, I can't tell you how sorry I am. I didn't mean to hurt anybody. But I guess I hurt you all."

I wiped at my eyes. "Christ, here we are like a couple of old ladies, sobbing and weeping at our reunion. We have to be more manly."

"Tears are manly, Roy. Go ahead and cry."

The crazy ping-ponging of emotions began to subside. "You did hurt everybody . . . but so what? You're a legend. And now you're a *living* legend." And that was all I had to say—"living"—and the tears came pouring out. I couldn't hold them back. They just spilled out of a well that had been quietly filling itself for all those years, and that well was now going to empty itself, right there, under the shade of Buddha's tree. And out they came: tears of anger, sorrow, loss and joy. I cried like a baby. The Poet squeezed my shoulder, and he began to cry. It was too much for him, too. And there we sat, the two of us, sobbing with relief, on a park bench, under the limbs of a great Bengali ficus, in the city of Victoria, on the island of Mahé, in the Seychelles, somewhere in the middle of the Indian ocean.

"We've got to stop this," the Poet said shakily through his tears and sniffles. "People are going to think we're drunk or something."

I laughed and cried at the same time, and my words came out all choked. "We are drunk, you asshole. We're a couple of old lady drunks . . . and we probably look ridiculous. But I don't care. You're alive." My shoulders shook as tears cascaded down my cheeks.

"Roy, come on . . . you're supposed to be the responsible one. You're the Apollonian half. I'm the volatile Dionysian. I get to cry my eyes out, not you."

"You just said it was good to cry, manly to cry." And I kept on weeping, spitting out the words. "I don't want to stop . . . " I laughed again, "it feels too good."

And he laughed. "Why do you think women do it?"

I laughed and sputtered and finally got myself under control. "Jesus, I haven't done that since I was a kid, but then it was from pain. This is like . . . joy and sorrow and . . . madness and gladness and . . .

"Feels good, doesn't it?"

"Man," I said, wiping the last of my tears away. "It's like an orgasm, or something."

"An emotional orgasm," he said as he wiped at his overflow. "The great release. One step shy of the release into the light."

That caught my attention and I wanted to hear more. "Release into the light? Are you talking mysticism?"

"I suppose so," he replied. "I'm talking about the energy. The light. That's what I found, after I left here."

Now we were back to the story, and this was the part I really wanted to hear. The transformation of the Poet. "So you lived here in Victoria, for five years? Getting drunk?"

"Until I had my fill. And yes, that took about five years. As long as our career had lasted, that's how long I drank. Every day that I had been on stage was a day I had to wash away with alcohol. It was like a cleansing, a baptism of booze. I lived in a fog—I drank, I ate, I read books. I'd swim in the ocean, or rather, I'd fall into the ocean and I'd drink some more."

"And that's what you did for five years?" I asked.

"That was pretty much it. I spent a lot of time in the bars, a lot of time sleeping it off in my room, I'd read here in the park, and go to the beach and talk to the tourists. I kept in touch with the world that way, talking to the tourists. Lots of English, then French and Germans. Swedes, too. Gorgeous, the Swedish chicks. Ready to jump in the sack with the American 'beachcomber.' I was very exotic. I had all the sex I needed. And lots of free meals. Everyone was ready to buy the mysterious beach bum lunch or dinner. And my little room was cheap. I'll show you the hotel where I stayed when we walk back. *La Veille Rose*—the Old Rose. So I managed to stretch my money for a long time. Cheap room, free meals, free sex, and all the conversation I needed. Everyone, all the young people, anyway, spoke English—the lingua franca of the world.

"I felt comfortable living the vagabond life . . . and completely empty. I tried to fill my emptiness with drink. That was my only real expense. The booze, the goddamned booze. And it worked, for a while. Then, little by little, the emptiness could no longer be filled. The hole in my psyche was getting larger—larger than the alcohol's ability to fill it. I was falling into myself, into the hole of myself. The whole area from my heart to stomach was imploding. I was being sucked down into a whirlpool, with nothing at the bottom, only the ice. Dante's last circle of hell, with the devil frozen in ice. And I was well on my way to becoming the devil, the bearer of evil, frozen inside of himself, and locked out for all eternity."

He put his hands behind his head and stretched himself out, as if to exorcise the memory. And then he shuddered slightly. "I was slipping into hell, Roy. I was gradually being cut off from all living contact. And I realized that hell was not all fire and brimstone and burning and torture. Hell is the *absence* of contact. Hell is total isolation, a frozen, non-feeling state. An existence in which there is no intimacy with the warmth of life."

He looked about at the life in the park under the shade of Buddha's tree, and in the streets beyond. The casual, slowly evolving life of the people of the Seychelles. "See the people move? Each with a purpose, whether it's work or play. Coming and going at his or her own pace, that slow and casual pace of the tropics. That delicious, languid pace."

I looked out at the Seychelloise. "They just seem to glide, don't they?"

"Like angels," the Poet said.

And we watched the graceful swirl of life that danced about us, as an angel passed overhead, silencing us and warming us in our hearts.

The Poet came out of his brief reverie and continued: "I was locked out of that!" He swept his hand out in a broad gesture that included not only the tree-shaded square of Victoria, but the whole world. "I was on the outside, locked out. All that life, swirling around me, and I couldn't touch it. I was gradually losing all contact with existence. I was frozen in my psychic body. Getting more and more frozen as the days crept by. And I was in a panic. I was having profound anxiety attacks. The fear was creeping in on me. Like Allen Ginsberg when he wrote to William Burroughs about his *ayahuasca* trips."

"*The Yage Letters*," I said. "That's a great book."

"I wrote our song 'What Do You Fear' from those *Yage Letters*."

"I always loved that tune."

"I loved your funky organ. And the guitar player's James Brown take on the whole thing. Too cool."

"Well, shit, man. We're gonna do it again. Right?"

He thought for a moment, laying his head to the side, ear almost touching his shoulder, like he used to, very noncommittal. And then he smiled: "You know, I think I'd kind of like that, Roy."

"All right!" I exclaimed. "There's no reason not to. What's holding you back?"

"Only life, my friend . . . and death."

I shivered. He could still do it. He could send a cold chill down your spine that could freeze your gonads. The Snake Man, at it again. I pushed him with both hands. "Don't do that, man. You're too good at it." He frowned a question at me, and I said, "You know what I'm talking about. Don't do it."

He laughed, and said, "Just keeping in practice. You know, the bon mot."

I shook off the word "death" and continued my questioning. "So you've been drinking for five years, and you're having a complete breakdown. What did you do?"

"Well, one morning I woke up with the usual hangover and went down to the beach to fall into the water. It was the best hangover remedy I'd found. Falling into warm salt water. Sure beats weird hot-sauce and bitters in tomato juice concoctions, hands down. A total immersion in our mother, the ocean. The waters of the womb . . . the Jungian unconscious. So I hit that water, and that's where I went. This poor, lost, drunken, abandoned, frozen soul finally dove into itself. I went under the water, came up, rolled on my back, looked up at the high blue sky and realized that the vast emptiness of that blue canopy was a reflection of the emptiness in my heart. And then I opened up. My heart just opened itself and I began to drift up into that sky. Floating on my back, hung over, in the Indian

Ocean, I sort of floated up out of my body, into the air and I saw that I *was* the sky. I *was* the air. And I let go of everything. I went into a rapture. Floating in the air and floating on my back in the ocean—spirit and matter at one and the same time. God, it felt good! And then I rolled over in the water face down, and I realized that the water was the sky, and *I* was the water. It was all one! And I dove down into my mother. Into the womb again. And when I came up and broke the surface of that soft, warm liquid, I was as refreshed as I had ever been in my entire life. Then my spirit floated back down into my body, down out of the air, out of its rapture. It re-entered its vessel, through my heart . . . and I was whole again. Reborn!"

He stopped speaking, and his eyes brightened, clear and lustrous. He was back there, in that memory. In the air. Enraptured.

I waited for him to come back out of his high. He had an almost beatific smile on his face that bespoke a knowledge beyond the ordinary. It was as if he had gained access to a secret, and that secret filled him with delight. And for a brief moment he was in that space again. In that secret knowledge. And I wanted to know what it was and how he had acquired it.

I had to call him back: "So that's what did it?" I asked. "That's what got you off the booze?"

He looked at me with those glowing blue eyes of his. "Roy, that moment was the beginning of the transformation. It's still going on, of course. But that immersion in the ocean started the whole damned thing."

10

So . . . what happened?" My curiosity was beyond containment.

"Well, basically, the Snake Man shed his skin." He took a deep breath. "I came out of that water a new man."

"Like a baptism," I said.

"Yes, but without the voodoo. This was the real thing. Just me, my soul, and I. The holy trinity . . . and the infinite. No words, no mumbo-jumbo, no magic show, no phony-baloney ceremony. No nothing. Only the elements. Earth, water, sky, and this now humble servant."

"And that was it?" I asked. "Simple as that . . . you'd changed?"

"Hell no. That was the first step of a thousand-mile journey. Coming up out of the water, I swam in to shore, and stepped onto the beach. The first step—not far from here, actually—of my long march. I walked across the beach, heading back to my hotel, and knew, in a flash, that I had to stop drinking. It was killing me. It no longer provided any pleasure or escape. I was like a junkie. I had to have my booze just to *maintain,* for chrissake. And you know what? The booze high, at its best, didn't even begin to compare to the experience I had just had. Floating in that ocean, I had caught a glimpse of eternity, and that was the only thing I wanted. I wanted to repeat that feeling, again and again. And I knew I sure as hell couldn't find it in a fucking bottle of bourbon. But I didn't know where it was. I didn't have the vaguest clue as to how to do it again."

"Did you ever find out?"

He grinned, the Cheshire cat at his ease. "Sure did, man."

"In the water?"

"Roy, I hit that water every day for the next two weeks. I stopped drinking cold turkey. Just like that. And whenever the nausea and the sweats and the shaking and the horror of the withdrawal came over me, I'd hit the ocean. I'd stagger down to the beach, just like on the day of my epiphany, and flop into the water. Then I'd swim out a bit and roll over on my back, and I'd stare at the sky, at the clouds. And nothing would happen. No lift-off—no transcendence. So I'd dive under the water, like I did that day. I'd hold my breath as long as I could, swimming down into the cool blue, waiting as long as I could. Nothing, man. I might as well have been waiting for Godot."

"'Mr. Godot can't come today.'"

"And he didn't," the Poet said. "I'd wheeze and strain and gird my loins . . . and nothing would happen. No, wait, that's not true. Something would happen. I'd throw up. I'd come up after holding my breath for as long as I could, break the surface . . . and throw up from the effort. I was like a whale floating in its own ambergris. And I'd feel rotten, floating in that gorgeous azure sea. Rotten, and scared, and lonely. And I thought to myself: 'What if I can't get that feeling back?' What if I can *never* get that feeling back? It's all I wanted. It had replaced everything. Booze, sex, literature, food. Everything! And I couldn't get back there. No matter how many times I floated on my back, staring into the sky, it wouldn't come. I wanted and wanted and wanted and it wouldn't come. I just couldn't regain that feeling of peace, no matter what I did."

"How did you solve the problem?" I asked. "Talk about paradise lost, you were living it."

"Eternity denied. Not a happy state of affairs. But at least I had stopped drinking. My head was clear again. Like on the beach in El Segundo when we first put the band together. Now I was on another beach, and it was time for another decision. It was life-altering time again. Time to make my move."

"To where?"

"To the mountains. But I didn't know it yet, not then."

"Where are they?" I asked.

"Hey, don't you want to know the chronology of events? You can't just leap ahead to the mountains without knowing how I got off the beach."

"All right. Finish the beach . . . then the mountains."

"And besides," he said, "You're going to like the end of the beach-bum/drunk phase of the Snake Man. Another shedding of the skin. This time by way of the Buddha."

"The Buddha?!"

"See, you like it already, don't you?"

"Of course," I said.

"So I'm on the beach, staring at the water, and it comes to me. Meditation. It was time for me to begin to meditate. Only I didn't know how. I didn't have the vaguest notion. I mean, what do you do? Sit under a tree? Like this?" He pointed up at the great, spreading limbs of the Bengali ficus, Buddha's tree. "Do you just sit here and think? And if so, about what? My life? Hell, that was fucked. I didn't need to think about that. I didn't need to think about all the wrong decisions I'd made; I just wanted to get away from my life, not review it. I didn't want to think about where I'd been. I wanted to figure out where I was going. And I wanted that to be into the blissful peace that I had experienced on that fateful day. I had to get back there. My life—my sanity—depended on it."

"So what did you do?"

"You'll love this. I did sit, right here under this tree. And I looked at this enormous trunk and these unbelievably broad spreading limbs. I studied every detail of the tree. And as I looked, a million thoughts came bubbling out of my memory storage banks. They just came flooding up, in bizarre, random combinations. Like bad surrealist poetry. And I didn't want to deal with any of them. It was all a rehash anyway, old junk that meant nothing. The deeds had already been done. I couldn't undo them, why dwell on them? So I walked on the beach and sat under this tree trying to clear my head, and one day the tree said to me: 'Why are you looking at me?'

"And I said to it: 'Because I need an answer.'

"'I don't have the answer,' the tree said. 'Not for you, anyway.'

"'But I need to know what to do.'

"'You shouldn't stay here anymore. You're a human, not a tree. You got to move, boy.'"

I smiled. "Spoke sort of like a Southerner, did it?"

The Poet laughed. "Yeah. Odd, isn't it? Who would think the Buddha tree would speak like that. Like an American from below the Mason-Dixon line. But that's what I heard it say. 'You got to *move*, boy!'

"So I started taking long walks on the beach. Moving and thinking, like under the tree. A kind of moving meditation. But nothing happened. And then one day a girl in cut-off jeans and a little bikini top—a girl of maybe fourteen—came walking down the beach towards me."

"Ah ha!" I said. "Once again, lust rears its moist and serpentine head."

"No, man. She was too young. But I must admit, she was intriguing. Tall, café-au-lait–tinted, but way too skinny, with nothing but little nubbin-breasts just beginning to sprout. Hardly any hips, either. But there was something in her eyes. A knowledge, perhaps. And she smiled at me. 'Why are you so sad on such a beautiful day, mister?' she said to me. Just like that."

"Out of the blue?" I asked.

"Yep, out of nowhere."

"You must have been dragging along like one sorry-ass specimen, my friend."

"That's just it, I wasn't. I was moving pretty smartly and feeling . . . well, not bad. Lost, but okay. And she just looked right through me. It was like she knew me and could see into my entanglement. I told her I wasn't sad but she insisted that I was, and that I was wasting a beautiful day."

"I'm sure she was right."

"She was, of course. And then she fell into step beside me, and I'll be damned if I didn't unburden myself to that little girl. I told her about my drinking and then my experience in the ocean. She understood the beauty of that moment. 'You married the sky, mister.' she said. Wasn't that poetic?"

"I like it," I said. "You married the sky."

"And I told her how I wanted to do it again. How I *had* to do it again. I told her I had been sitting under Buddha's tree *trying* to do it again. She looked at me, into my eyes, and smiled like a flower. 'Then why don't you go to the Buddha?' she said."

"What did she mean?"

"That's what I asked her. She said, 'Well, you've been sitting under the Buddha's tree and that hasn't worked for you. Why don't you go to the Buddha . . . to India? There are many holy men in India. Perhaps one of them can help you.' And it was like, Eureka! Why didn't I think of that? She had the answer. This too-tall, too-skinny, café-au-lait Seychelloise girl of barely fourteen had the answer. I laughed and gave her a great big hug. Spun her around in the air a few times—she squealed like a puppy—I said, '*Merci beaucoup, mon amour.*' and ran off to find my destiny."

"Just like that?'

"Why not? I packed my bag, got some traveler's checks, checked out of The Old Rose, and bought a plane ticket."

"Whoa, a plane ticket? To where?"

"To India, Roy. Delhi, the capital—New Delhi and Old Delhi. The heart of the matter. I figured I'd go to the capital city and see what I could find in the way of . . . "

"A guru?" I had to jump in. I couldn't imagine the Poet sitting at the feet of a teacher.

"Well . . . yeah. A guru, I guess. At least someone to push me in the right direction."

"And did you find one?"

"In Delhi I found everything . . . and nothing. It was teeming and bustling and swarming. Modern and ancient at the same time. Young businessmen in suits and ties and attaché cases, talking high finance as a cow or two walked down the street and beggars with sad, hungry eyes held their hands out for spare change amidst a swirl of garbage. Dogs rooting in the garbage, people living in cardboard boxes next to the garbage heaps which were next to the quite fine houses of wealthy Delhi entrepreneurs. Cars and trucks and busses jamming the roads, with ox carts and the occasional elephant slowing the whole wave down to a crawl. New construction, old ruins, beautiful temples, terrible slums. Gorgeous women in saris, crippled old hags, bigshot politicians in limos and thousands of starving children begging, stealing and scraping by, clinging to life with a fierce tenacity. From the high to the low. A monstrous hodgepodge of humanity."

"Don't tell me you found a guru in the midst of all of that," I said.

He shook his head 'no.' "I found the *sadhus*," he said.

"The hoodoos?"

He laughed. "Almost. The sadhus, the holy men. But they were like hoodoos. They're these almost naked guys with beards and begging bowls and white ash all over their bodies and prayer beads around their necks and the most incredible stoned look in their eyes. They're like kief masters. Stoners of the highest order. Men on the road, on the trail of Vishnu."

"The sadhus on the trail of Vishnu were like hoodoos?"

"Hey, that's not bad. It's got a rhythm to it. Like Sanskrit rap. I think you've got something there. You're becoming 'M.C. Rhymin' Roy.'" And he crooked his head, as if he were hearing something in his mind's ear. Something new, that was inspiring him. "Vishnu and the sadhus got the hoodoo! Get the drummer to put a beat to that and we're rockin'!" He slapped at his thighs, beating out a little rhythm, and repeated the words: "Vishnu and the sadhus got the hoodoo. And the Gita got the Shiva and the Brahma." He laughed, his eyes lit up—he was seeing into the future—and he leaned toward me. "That's the start of our comeback, man. Our first silly ditty. We could bring them some kundalini and the *Bhagavad Gita* and some Tibetan Buddhism and toss in a Zen koan or two and stir up the dharma and put some sitar-guitar and your ice-jazz chords over a good, solid tabla-rock beat and we're there. In a new place, with our new music!"

And just like that he had divined our new direction. He wanted to do this! He felt the surge again. The old desire for music and singing was welling up in him. He would spin his words again, his new words over our new music.

"Roy, man. We're gonna do some raga rock and roll!" He jumped up from his seat and did his American Indian hop dance, his trademark move—the Snake Man on stage. He was being transformed right before my eyes. The shapeshifter was shedding decades. In his mind's eye he was back in the center of the maelstrom—the rock and roll madness of our first go-around. And people were screaming, the music was blaring, the lights were flashing and twirling and spinning in their delirious kaleidoscope, and the security guards were ready for mayhem, ready for a riot. It was pandemonium. And he was there. Smiling and hopping and hearing our new music in his head.

That was when I knew I could take him back to the States and the four of us would reunite to work the magic again. I was deliriously happy.

"I love this direction," I said. "I've always wanted to play Indian improvisations with the other two guys. We only did 'The Ending Tone,' and that wasn't nearly enough. I want more!"

"Me too," the Poet said. "I could float a lot of stories over those Indian beats. Man, I haven't sung in far too long a time. I miss it, and now that I'm with you, I realize just how much. Shit, man, I feel inspired."

"Me too," I said, smiling broadly.

We paused for a beat, and then the Poet took in a deep breath and smiled broadly. "See, it *is* good for brethren to dwell together in harmony."

"Amen, brother. Now tell me what happened with the sadhus. Did you become one of them?"

He sat back down on the bench. "No, that's their own trip," he said. "I don't think a white boy from Los Angeles could really become one of them. It's indigenous to the Indian subcontinent. It's theirs and no one else's. I have seen a few English seekers trying to emulate them . . . didn't work, though. The sadhus are just too Indian. But I did hang out with them."

"Doing what? Begging?"

He laughed. "No, mainly talking. And smoking ganja. Man, those guys could smoke a lot of weed. Like Rastafarians, religious heads. But they were on the search for the mystic. They had given up everything. They had no possessions and had to live by their wits. Some of them were charlatans—that's where the hoodoo comes in. Some of them were psychotics, and the ganja really didn't help. If anything, it intensified their derangements. But most were seekers. Honest, pot-smoking seekers. And I wanted to learn from them. So I talked with them—at least the ones who could speak English. And there were enough. They told me stories from the holy books: the *Upanishads*, the *Bhagavad Gita*, the *Vedas*; and stories of the Buddha and Krishna the blue god. They filled my head with mythic tales of battles and lovers, sacrifice and renunciation . . . and *samadhi*."

"I don't know that word."

"Samadhi is the whole ball game. The goal of our existence. The French would say our *raison d'être*. Of course they don't apply that phrase to the inner life. For them, and for just about all of us, the reasons for being are ultimately mundane, of-this-world, three-dimensional."

And then the Poet went silent. He just sat there, as if he were contemplating some inner vision, eyes half-closed, not moving, barely breathing.

Finally, I had to speak. I had to call him back from wherever he was in his mind. "So what does it mean already?" I asked.

He didn't move. Those sexy, sleepy lids of his, the ones the girls loved in our performing days, stayed at half-mast. He was gone somewhere else.

"Hey! You're not alone here, you know." I almost shouted at him.

And he came out of it, back to the mundane. "Oh yes I am, Roy."

I didn't understand. "What are you talking about?"

"We are alone. All alone. Just you . . . and me. And of course everything else that exists." Then he chuckled to himself. "And everything that doesn't exist, too."

"Now I really don't understand," I said.

He smiled, "And everything that may exist, and everything that has existed. Alone. All of it. Alone."

"How can that be? We're here. We're not alone. We're surrounded by things and people and life. And the sky and the sun and this tree we're sitting under. How can we be alone?"

"Because it's all one!" He chuckled again. "How does that song go? 'One is the loneliest number that you'll ever do.'"

"Yeah. I remember that song. So what?"

"Well, one is not the loneliest number; it's the greatest

number. Everything is one! And the one is the all. We're at once here and infinite. And so is everything else. And it's all one, and nothing. And it's all me, because I made it up."

"Come on, man. Don't tell me you've become a megalomaniac. What do you mean you made it up?"

"Actually, Roy, you made it up."

"Me?"

He let out a big, roaring belly laugh. A laugh that came from deep within him and went rolling up and out at the world. It hit me in the chest, that roar of laughter, and it made my heart feel warm and safe.

"Yes, you, amigo," he said after his laughter subsided. "You are the creator. You made up this whole damned thing!"

"Me?"

"Well, you and me. Because I'm the creator, too. We made it up. All of it. And I like it, don't you? We did a damn fine job."

"You and me?" I was dumbfounded. What the hell was he talking about?

"Well, actually, everyone else, too." He gestured at the passing parade of Victoria. "They all had a hand in this existence."

"How?"

"Don't you see? All of this is the mind of the creator. And we, our collective mind, are the mind of the creator. We are all one with the creator . . . ergo, we *are* the creator."

"How do you know we are all one with the creator?"

"Didn't you ask me to explain samadhi?"

"Yes, and you didn't answer me."

"I just did."

And he grew silent again. He sat there and stared off, beyond everything. I felt that if I didn't speak, we might sit there silently for the next six months.

"You're giving me the riddle of the Sphinx," I said. "Some kind of esoteric conundrum."

A smile crept across his face. "The *mysterium aeternum*. The secret knowledge. The *arcanum*." His grin broadened and he seemed to be taking great delight in my confusion.

"I'm not giving you a riddle," he continued. "I'm giving you the answer."

"To what?" I said. "To samadhi, or to the mystery of existence?"

"Yes, exactly."

"Come on, man. Which one?"

"Both!" He shouted. And then he laughed again. This was just too much fun for him.

"Stop laughing," I said. "I'm not enjoying this."

"Why?" he managed, through gulps of air.

"Because you're having way too good of a time, and at my expense."

"Roy, laughter is the cure for what ails us. It's the great healing balm. It's the holy oil that the Father allows us to pour over ourselves to cleanse and refresh us. To wash away our sorrows, our deep humiliation, our pains and sufferings. If we didn't have laughter we'd go mad. We take ourselves too seriously as it is. We need to lighten up. We need to immerse ourselves in the light . . . and we need to laugh. You need to laugh, Roy. You're way too poker-faced, too heavy."

He was right, I was too serious. I'd always been that way. But in our youth, in the days of our band, he was the excessively serious one. There was no laughter from the Poet back then. He was gravitas itself. And now, here he was, roaring with deep belly-laughs. And I wanted to know what had caused the change. How had he become this man of humor, this chortling sphinx?

"And by the way," he said. "I'm not laughing at you. I'm just glad to be alive, know what I'm saying? Because for so long I didn't know what it meant to be alive."

"How did you find out?"

"That's what I'm trying to tell you. Now, let's see, where were we?"

"The riddle."

"Ah, yes . . . samadhi. The goal, the point of this existence. And here's the riddle part—the obliteration of this existence. It's both the goal and beyond comprehension. It's the great understanding and beyond reason. It's the all, and it's not a damned thing."

"How am I supposed to understand this?"

"It's in all of us. Hell, it *is* all of us. It's nirvana. It's the bliss that the Beatles' Maharishi used to talk about. It's Jesus saying 'I and the Father are one.' It's the Hebrew dictum 'Hear, oh Israel, the Lord God is One.' It's the *kether* of the Kabbalah, the crown of the *Sephiroth*. It's the *an-Nur*, the light, of Islam. It's the ineffable Tao of China. It's the Native American's *Wakan Tanka*." And then he laughed again. "It's the big taco."

I had to laugh with him. It was just too goofy - "the big taco." And there we sat under Buddha's tree, two aging hippies, laughing at the world and laughing at ourselves.

"And you got all of this from the sadhus? The hoodoo-voodoo men that you hung out with in Delhi?"

"Oh no. They were just the guys who set me on the path. They were the ones who told me I had to go into the mountains. To Rishikesh."

11

S o off I went," the Poet said, "to find the holy mountain. Into the foothills of the Himalayas, where the Ganges begins. It comes down out of the mountains and at Rishikish its waters are fresh and pure, all bubbling green and topped with white foam as it races over the granite rocks and boulders. Then it moves on and down to the plains of Uttar Pradesh, one of the Northern states, and winds its way East across the country, merging with other tributaries, and then it dips south, to the bay of Bengal, where it fans out into a great alluvial flood plain.

"They call the river *Ganga-Ma*, Mother Ganges. It represents the source of life and holiness. The waters are purifying, cleansing, rejuvenating. One of the goals of all Indians is to bathe at least one time in the Ganges. And they come to four holy places to do it, in twelve-year cycles, rotating once every three years to the cities of Allahabad, Haridwar, Ujjain, and Nasik. They have a great festival called the *Kumbah Mela,* and millions of people, especially the sadhus, come to take a holy bath in Ganga-Ma to wash their sins away and purify their souls. The sadhus wear virtually nothing; many of them go naked but for garlands of beautiful golden marigolds around their necks. And they come en masse, and plunge themselves into the river, and there is much singing and music and drumming and dancing from everyone in attendance. It's an amazing gathering of humanity, all colorful and joyous and cleansing.

"And I actually witnessed it. In Haridwar, which means the Gates of God, on my way further up into the mountains. I was overwhelmed by the sight of all those white ash–covered sadhus. The power of those guys. Man, I'm telling you, you could feel it coming off of them. They had plugged into something, and I wanted to know what it was. I just wanted to get back there, to that moment in the water when I left myself and merged with the sky. And there I was in Northern India, in the city of Haridwar, and it was the water again. I was going to immerse myself in the water, in that holy, purifying water. I was not in the middle of the Indian Ocean anymore. I was on the banks of the Ganges . . . and I just jumped in with them. I stripped off all my clothes, put them in a little pile, and hit the water with the sadhus. God it was cold! That clear, fresh Ganga-Ma was mountain water. I'm talking cold, man. I was in—and I was out! And the holy men *loved* it. This obviously Western, European white boy, buck naked, freezing his lily-white ass off, drew howls of laughter from the sadhus.

"But I had immersed myself. That was what mattered to me. I quickly dressed, and they were slapping me on the back and laughing and chatting amongst themselves. Then they broke out the peace pipe. The *chillum*, they called it. And we all smoked some *charas*. Hashish. Passing the chillum around is one of their rituals. They consider it a kind of food of the gods."

I had to laugh. "So do we," I said.

"They love their hash," he said. "They're holy stoners on the path, like we were in the '60s. Like so many people were back then. And then somehow we lost it. A whole generation just lost its direction and went materialistic."

"What do you think happened?" I asked.

"I don't know, man. All I know for sure is that in my case it was the booze. I lost myself in a bottle of Kentucky bourbon. But there I was, in Northern India, beside Mother Ganges, freezing my ass off and smoking hashish with a bunch of Indian holy men—the hoodoo sadhus. And I was going to find my way back. I was going to reclaim myself. No more slave to the booze. No more slave to anything. I was back on the path." And then he smiled. "I was back in the saddle again."

"The Snake Man rides!" I said. And we both laughed.

"The *Naga Babas* are the real snake men. The Nagas are the sort of militant branch of the sadhus. And *naga* is the snake, the cobra. They're always naked—they say they're not naked, but clad in the sky—and they carry a trident. It looks like a weapon, and it was a weapon in the old days, but the three blades—they kind of look like horns—represent the Hindu trinity: Brahma, the creator; Vishnu, the preserver; and Shiva, the destroyer. And man, when the Nagas came to bathe in the river on that holy day . . . look out! They came in a rush and a ruckus and *everybody* got out of their way. They're into all kinds of ascetic weirdness, most of it way too much for West Coast city boys like you and me. But I must say, I was intrigued—Snake Man to snake men."

"Did you spend any time with them?" I asked.

"Naw, not really. They wouldn't allow it, although they were friendly enough. They just didn't have any time for pilgrims. Or apprentices. That's what the *ashrams* were for. And that's where they said I should go."

"To Rishikesh," I said.

"Yeah. That's where the schools are, the communities. An ashram's like a hermitage. A place where a teacher, a guru, instructs students and disciples. They said go to Rishikesh and enter an ashram."

I still couldn't imagine the Poet as a student sitting at the feet of a teacher. He was far too independent, too much of an individualist to subscribe to any kind of codified teaching.

"So what did you do? Did you actually find a guru and enter an ashram?"

He stretched his limbs. "Well . . . not really. But yes . . . and then again, no."

It was riddle-of-the-sphinx time again. "Now what is *that* supposed to mean?" I asked jokingly.

"Well, it's not really the point of the story, but let me try to make it seem like, in retrospect, I had some idea of what I was doing. I set off walking—it was only about twenty-five miles—with my duffel bag slung over my shoulder and my notebook at the ready."

"Notebook? Did you make a record of your journey? Do you have the notebook?"

He laughed. "The answer to all of those questions is 'no.' Oh, I did take a few notes. Jotted down some local color and my thoughts, but the local color is always there, and my thoughts were like a tree full of squirrels. Jumping and chittering and jabbering."

I interrupted him: "Let me guess. You threw the damned thing away, right?"

He tucked in his head as if flinching from a blow and grinned. "Actually, I tore out the few pages I'd written on and gave the notebook and my neat pen to a little kid. He dug it. You know what he said to me. 'Groovy!' Even in India, the kids said 'groovy.' They're all the same, you know? Computers and CDs and movies—the kids are all the same. I tell you, one world is coming, Roy. The electronic age is making this into one world. Of course it's one world already, but most of us don't know that. But we will find out, and when we do . . . well, 'groovy!'"

"So you just threw the pages away," I said, remembering the notebooks of our youth. "Again."

"Yep . . . on the road to Rishikesh. I sat down one evening, read what I had written, and bagged it. I wasn't looking to write a journal, I was looking for the sky. I wanted to dive into the light. I had to have that release again, and I was going to have it, or die trying. I had nothing else. I had left everything else behind. This was it, my journey to the East, my existential moment. I was at the crossroads, and the road led to Rishikesh.

"And lord, what a beautiful road it was. Giant conifers and North Indian indigenous trees. So green and lush and bursting with life. Fine, sweet air, so good in the lungs. Great, huge boulders, like fortresses. The Himalayas off in the distance, framing every view to the north with a sprinkle of white powder on the peaks. And Ganga-Ma, rushing and tumbling down, oxygenating the air, all fresh and clean.

"I tell you, Roy . . . I felt good on that trek. I was really starting to feel alive. Something—I didn't know what—was up there, waiting for me. I would have loved to have just sat by the river, my back against a tree, like Bob Dylan 'watching the river flow,' and just looked out at the beauty of the whole damned thing. It was that wonderful. But I was on a journey, a pilgrimage, and I had to get there. A pilgrim's gotta move. You can't be on a search and just sit on your ass enjoying the scenery. So I picked up the pace and continued on to Rishikesh.

"I walked along the Ganges, breathing the air, and I finally came to the town. A charming place, small but with everything I would need. Bookstore, restaurants, post office, little hotels, shops, food stands . . . everything. There were all kinds of houses running up into the hills where the people lived, and where the ashrams were. Or so I supposed. But how to find them? I couldn't read Sanskrit. I didn't see any signs in English saying: 'Ashrams this way.' So I asked some town folks, but of course they didn't speak English. I was getting very frustrated. Here I was, the Snake Man, practically at the roof of the world, in a holy town by the holy river, looking for a teacher, a guru, and I couldn't even figure out how to find an ashram. So I just plopped down on the side of the road and sat there. I figured I'd get an idea, or something would happen. Roy, I didn't know what I was doing. But at least I was there. I wasn't the drunk anymore. I wasn't the rock star anymore. I really wasn't the Snake Man anymore. I had shed that skin of my youth and I was hoping to become a new man. But how? When I couldn't even find an ashram.

"So I sat on my ass, an American in India, In the state of Uttar Pradesh, a million miles from home—although I didn't even *have* a home anymore. I was a dead man. I had died in Paris, and I was free. And completely lost.

"And sitting there, at the side of the road, with the midday sun shining down on me, I began to have a nervous breakdown. I began to dissolve inside myself. My nerves would no longer support my energy body. All the years of dissipation caught up to me, right there, in Rishikesh, just South of the Ram Jhula bridge. A great fear swept over me and my heart started pumping blood through my body at an insane rate. I began shaking, and the more I shook the more the fear sunk its teeth into me, biting me in the chest and stomach, tearing away my resolve, my courage. I was being consumed by the demon of fear. It was a terrible moment. I couldn't move. I could hardly breathe. I was hyperventilating, gasping for air. I had never experienced such anxiety, such a bottomless sinking feeling. It was like a whirlpool had started spinning inside of me and was sucking me into my solar plexus. And I couldn't climb back out. I was being devoured by my own ego, and the demon of fear."

The Poet was breathing hard, now, perspiration beading on his brow. "Those two always travel together," he continued in a rush. "But the ego dominates our everyday lives. And we're always trying to fill it because it's always hungry and it always wants something. Fame, money, power, dominance, control—those are the things it loves, and it wants as much as it can get. I mean, it's fine, it makes sense to want a decent life and a shot at happiness. To have a little job, and a family, and a roof over our heads, and a car, and a little money in the bank to feed our little family, our wife and kids.

"And everything would be fine if we could stop there. But we can't! We always want more. That's the true human condition—to want more. To fill our egos to the bursting point because we don't know we exist. We think we *are* our egos. We think we are Roy, and we think we are the newly minted Joseph K. Phoenix, and we have to constantly feed those entities with psychic dominance in order to justify our own existence. All the stuff we want to acquire and all the power trips we lay on each other flow out of our animal nature. We're like beasts with the gimmies. We've got to have it all. But with the gimmies comes the fear. Because if we finally get it, we're afraid of losing it. And with the 'I want' comes the terror. The ego, the unique me on the inside, is always terrified of falling apart. And if it dissolves, if it does fall apart, there goes us! Roy is gone. Joseph K. is gone. And that's the ultimate terror. Or so I thought back then.

"And that terror did descend on me. By the roadside in Rishikesh, my ego gave out. I had bloated it beyond all recognition, and it finally exploded. All the fame, drugs, sex, adulation, limos, food, girls, photographers, VIP rooms, planes, hotels, magazine covers, private parties, opening night premieres and big, big bucks . . . detonated! I was left with nothing. That's when fear realized it was time to make its move. The ego defenses had been shattered, and it was just what the thousand-headed demon was waiting for. Fear rushed in and began devouring me.

"I was cold, and terrified, and shaking, and alone, and trying my damnedest not to cry. I hadn't cried since my father beat me for stealing some candy when I was, like, eight or nine. I swore then that I would never let that son of a bitch, or anyone, ever see me cry again. And there I was, the oh-so-successful rock star, sniveling like a child on the side of the road. What a sham my stardom was. What a sham my *life* was. And I realized all the lies as the fear engulfed me."

I could feel the Poet's great anguish in the retelling of that terrible moment of dissolution. "What did you do? I mean, everything must have resolved itself. After all, here you are, alive and sane."

He smiled and stretched himself luxuriously. "An angel came to me, Roy. An angel."

He let that statement hang in the air as he stood and did a kind of stretch. He put his hands behind his back, clasped them together and bent forward from the waist. His head almost touched his shins and he raised his arms up behind his back, to such an extent that I was certain he would dislocate his shoulders. I was amazed at his suppleness. The stretch seemed incredibly difficult and yet here he was, a man in his late fifties, flowing into it with ease and grace.

"Where did you learn that stretch?" I said as he came back up and released his arms from their tortuous conceit. "It's like a crane standing on its head."

"I like that, Roy. A crane . . . yes. I'm going to call it the 'Sandhill Crane' from now on. For you, and for Audubon's *Birds of America*."

"Wasn't he an artist?" I asked.

"That's right, he did a painting or drawing of every single bird of America. And they're incredibly beautiful. I especially love his sandhill crane from the Florida coast. A magnificent bird, all legs and wings, with a bit of red on its crown. As if its crown chakra had burst into flame. You can see the energy radiating from its head. And that's what I'm going to think of whenever I stretch out in this particular *asana*. You, and Audubon, and the energy."

"So where did you learn how to do that?"

He sat back down, "In India, Roy. Courtesy of my angel."

"Tell me about the angel."

"All right, but let me go at my own pace. I haven't thought about this stuff in a long time, and your being here gives me a chance to talk it all out. And it's kind of fun, you know."

He closed his eyes and drew in a breath.

After a long pause he said, "Isn't it funny the shapes the spirit can take in your hour of need? This angel that came to me in my darkest hour came in the shape of a little boy not more than ten years old. He wore shorts, sneakers, and a T-shirt that read, 'Led Zeppelin.' And he was an angel. He squatted down beside me, took my hand, and in delightfully accented English said, 'Are you okay, mister? Do you need help?' I looked into his eyes. And I knew everything was going to work out. An angel from Zeppelin's *Houses of the Holy* had come to save me. And then the tears came pouring out of me. I couldn't hold them back anymore. Tears of relief just came streaming out of my eyes and down my cheeks. The little angel blotted at them with his incongruous T-shirt. I mean, come on . . . Led Zeppelin in the middle of Rishikesh? But didn't we always intend rock and roll to be a new universal language? Well, it had become just that. And here was the proof—my angel.

"After he blotted my tears away, and I began to regain my composure, he very gently pulled me up to my feet, and in the sweetest voice, said: 'Please come with me, mister. I know what you want.' He took my hand, delicately, gracefully, and began to lead me down the road. I followed him without any resistance. I felt perfectly secure in whatever destination he had in mind. This little rock-and-roller had my destiny in his hands and I completely trusted him to make the right choice. His energy, his vibrations were so sweet and pure that I knew he had been sent for me. Or he had been watching out for me. They say the guru appears when the student is ready."

"This was your guru? " I asked. "This little boy was going to be your teacher?"

The Poet laughed. "No, man. He was the messenger, my

guide. This was my Virgil, who had come to lead me through
the Inferno and set me on the path of freedom. And as we
walked along the roadside, his little hand in mine, a great bur-
den began to lift from me. I began to feel good deep inside, in
that hollow cavity of dread that had opened in me as far back as
our third album together. The emptiness began way back then,
maybe even further back. And it had gradually widened, with
my drinking and craziness, until it completely engulfed me, and
I fell into it—into the terror—right there in Rishikesh. But now
a strange happiness was starting to spread through me.

"'You like rock and roll, mister?' the angel said to me after we
had walked in silence for about three or four blocks.

"I had to smile to myself. The irony of it all. Roy, I hated rock
and roll. It's what took me into all the insanity. It was directly
responsible for my madness, for my terror, for my drinking. But
I loved it, too. I loved everything we did together. I loved the
music we made. I loved singing over your keyboards, and the
drums and guitar. We were great together. And I loved it."

I had to interrupt again. "Hey, rock and roll didn't cause the
fear in you. You did."

"I know that now," the Poet said. "But at that instant, with an
angel's hand in mine, I hated rock and roll. It was responsible,
not me. But as soon as I had that thought, that blame-laying
thought, I knew that I was wrong. The realization that I was
ducking the responsibility for my own actions just swept over
me. I loved rock and roll because it had brought me to that particular place in space and time, where I felt I was about to dis-
cover just who I really was.

"I said to that little angel: 'I love rock and roll.' And he said to
me, in a voice that sounded like bells, 'Me too, mister. It's
bitchin'!' And I almost started to cry again. My heart was filled

to overflowing with love for that little angel when he said 'It's bitchin'!' it was almost more than I could take. I fought back the tears and I said to him, 'Where are we going, son?'

"And he stopped, looked up at me, and said: 'We are here, mister. This is it.'"

12

Yellow painted buildings lined either side of the road, the road to Lakshman Jhula," the Poet continued. "And they were of that beautiful saffron yellow that you see all over India. My little angel said to me: 'You go here, mister.' And he pointed to a gate that led into a cluster of saffron houses gathered around a garden. 'Go in', he said. 'They will know what to do. This is the school of Sivananda.'

"'Will I see you again?' I asked my angel. 'Sure, mister', he said. 'If you stay.' And he laughed his little bell tones at me. 'We can talk rock and roll. I live here in Rishikesh.' And he turned and slipped off, almost as if he were floating. 'Bye mister!'

he called back to me as he disappeared around a corner and was gone.

"I stood in the middle of the street, not sure of what to do, and then I hiked up my courage and went in. To Sivananda's ashram. To my future.

"It was both peaceful and busy at the same time. There was a lot of coming and going. People of all ages were moving about—young men, middle-aged men, older men, and a scattering of women. They seemed very purposeful and yet very light in their movements. Everything was infused with a lightness, a grace and a sense of joy. I felt good being there. I felt I belonged there, and could learn something. I thought I might come to realize who I was at that saffron ashram.

"Then I saw a pillar in the courtyard. I went up to take a look, and saw that it was a list of twenty instructions from the founder, Swami Sivananda, inscribed in English. I stood there, very slowly reading and digesting what each instruction might mean."

"Did you understand them? Did they make any sense to you?"

"Yes, they did. Do you want to hear them?"

"Sure. Can you still remember them?"

"I think so," he said. "We had to memorize them. Part of our discipline, our mind control.

"They went something like this:

1. Up at four A.M. Do mantra meditation.
2. Sit in lotus posture, if possible.
3. Eat good balanced food, and not too much. Lots of fruit and vegetables.
4. Do charity for others.
5. Read the holy books, every day.
6. Retain your vital essence . . . your semen.

7. Give up your anger, jealousy, delusions, passions, addictions.

8. Give up smoking, narcotics, intoxicants, drinking."

"Seven and eight are the hard ones," I said. "How the hell did you do it?"

"Quiet, man. I'm on a roll here. I can see the pillar. Don't break my train of thought."

He plunged in again:

"9. Fast on holy days, or take only a little milk and fruit.

10. Be silent for two hours a day."

"Another impossible one for you."

"Roy . . . shut up!

11. Speak the truth. Speak little, and sweetly.

12. Lead a simple, happy life.

13. Be kind to all. Hurt no one's feelings."

"Another tough one for you."

"Ha, funny.

14.Analyze yourself—I hated this one—your mistakes.

15. Be self-reliant and responsible.

16. Think of the creator when you wake and sleep.

17. Practice simple living and high thinking.

18. Serve the poor and the sick.

19. Keep a quiet place to meditate.

20. Stick to it!"

He smiled. "It all sounded like a possible plan, very organized. I wanted to do it, to stay there, to study. And then another angel came to me."

"Another kid?" I asked.

"Nope. This angel was an old man. And what dignity he had. What peace emanated from him. And light—he was practically glowing—and I was warmed by his presence. He looked deep into my eyes, as if he were reading my soul . . . and I suppose he was.

"He said: 'Can you do it? Can you follow the rules?'

"I looked into his radiant face and I knew I could do whatever he asked of me. I said 'Yes, father. I can.'

"I instinctively called him father. I didn't know who, or what he was, but I knew he was my father."

"Who was he?" I asked.

"He was called Krishnananda. He had been a disciple of the founder, Swami Sivananda, who had died in 1963. Now, Swami Krishnananda was in charge. And he ran a tight ship. He was a no-nonsense guy. Very blunt, yet very funny. Of course, I learned all this later. Sitting with him, listening to his lectures, asking him questions . . . man, he tore me apart. Cut right to the quick. He always had me reading something, always encouraged me to ask questions. And then when I did, he'd cut up my Snake Man persona. He was trying to reduce who I was, the rock star who came to India, to zero."

"So you stayed?" I asked.

"Yes, he let me join the ashram. And he let me begin the search that brought me back to where I started. To the man that I always was. Who I hadn't yet known.

"And what a tortuous route it was. Filled with disciplines to whip this one-time reprobate into physical, moral, and spiritual shape. There were meditations and chantings in the early morning; yoga postures, what they call asanas; and breathing techniques, or *pranayama*. There were hours, endless hours of quiet sitting with the word *yam* going around in my head like a trapped and buzzing bee, obliterating all thought and quieting, or trying to quiet my monkey-mind. I swear, Roy, my mind was like a little circus monkey locked in a cage. It was always squealing and howling and bouncing around on itself. It would never shut up. I was always reliving past incidents, either joyful or painful. I'd remember hurting somebody, saying something snotty or sarcastic, and feeling so smug about it at the time it happened. Then—in my meditation—I'd beat myself up over it, I'd be ashamed of myself. And then I realized that I could never undo the pain I'd caused, and that hurt me deeply. I would always have to carry the pain with me. Even if I were to say 'I'm sorry' to that person, it still wouldn't eradicate, it still wouldn't *reverse* that moment."

The Poet shook his head and his smile was sad. "Here I was supposed to be meditating, supposed to be clearing my mind. And instead, I was piling up sin after sin into this mountain of regret.

"But then the pleasurable memories came back. The good times, the loves, the sex. Especially the sex! I was horny as hell. But one of the rules was retention of semen. So, no sex—not even wet dreams. You could actually begin to control that, if you were practiced. But the thoughts came anyway. I'd be in the middle of meditation and I'd be balling some groupie after one of our concerts. Man, what a distraction!

"And then I'd think about our music, and how good it was, and what fun we had, and how we had conceived of the whole thing on the beach in El Segundo, and how we made all the imaginings become a reality. God, I loved that. We were so young and pure and innocent. And then I went mad. Mad with the fame and power, the worship and the adulation. Mad with control. The control of the minds and will and even the destinies of other people."

I had to make him see that things could be different. "But this time you don't have to do that. You're in control of yourself now.

We can just make music for the sheer joy of it. Just for the delight of the four of us locking into the rhythm and flowing with the chord changes and you floating over the top of our foundation, spinning out your new skein of words."

We paused for a moment, imagining our new reality, and then the Poet spoke. "I like the sound of that, Roy. I've been wanting to make music with you guys for a long time. I really miss it."

"So do I, amigo. So do I." I could feel it. We were going to make music again, and it was going to be better than ever. But as much as I wanted to drift off into the future, I was pulled back to his story "So how did you get out from under that mountain of sin?" I asked. "How did you tame the monkey?"

The Poet took in a deep breath of air, held it, and slowly released it. I heard a hissing sound, like a snake. And then he spoke. "The physical postures, the asanas, are what helped do it. The bends and twists, and the headstands, *sirshasana* they call it. We'd start every day with a series of postures to stretch and warm the body, and a devotion to the sun. The whole ashram would greet that great golden orb with *Surya Namaskara*, the Sun Salutation. We'd face the East—its rising—and bathe our whole bodies in the life-giving rays of the morning sun, that giver of light and energy and warmth to the whole world. We'd do a round of twelve postures, and each round would have a little prayer of honor to the sun, a repeating of the twelve names of the Lord of the Sun. We'd say: 'All honor to Him who is the luminous power of love, the cause of all change, to Him who inspires all activity, who brings forth the light, who moves across the sky, who nourishes all, who is all wealth, who is within the rays, who is worthy of all worship, who is the sustainer of all things, who is the son of *Aditi* the mother of infinite consciousness, and who is the cause of all illumination.'

"And we'd do the twelve postures twelve times, flowing from one to another in smooth, graceful movements. Stretching out our stiffness, lubricating our joints, elongating our muscles. It was very easy but it generated a lot of internal heat. I loved it, and I still do it every morning.

"Swami Krishnananda would tell us: 'The Sun is the most life-giving force on the planet. It is the visual representation of the invisible Almighty. Man cannot think of the transcendent Supreme Absolute without the help of an object, and the Sun is the best object for worship and meditation. I love *Surya,* the Sun. It is the beautiful lord of the world, the absolute knowledge, the ever-pure, the golden consciousness, the crest-jewel. It is the very heart of the forms of the holy trinity of Brahma, Vishnu and Shiva. It is the giver of light. Just feel it!' And he would tilt his head back, close his eyes, and let the sun shine on his face. And I'll be damned if the sweetest little smile didn't creep across his face, turning that old curmudgeon into a child again. For a brief moment, our yogic taskmaster revealed the true nature within himself. And Roy, it was a little child. A sweet little boy smiling into the sun. And I'd look at him with such envy. That was what I wanted. To become that innocent, loving child again. To feel the way I felt when I was, like, seven or eight years old."

"Didn't Jesus say, 'To enter the kingdom of heaven you must become like a child?' " I asked the Poet.

"Exactly. And you must be born again. Into the light."

"Did you ever see the little angel again?"

"Sure. In Rishikesh. I'd go into town for this or that. Soap, razor blades, an English newspaper, a snack of Indian sweets. They had a little sweet shop . . . made great *gulabs* and *rasmalai.* Great *samosas,* too. And I'd be relaxing, eating my gulab, leaning against a building, and along would come my little angel. We'd talk, and then he'd take me to the river. I'd buy him a sweet or a savory, and we'd sit by the river and just watch it flow by, down from the Himalayas on its journey to the Bay of Bengal, a journey of a thousand miles. Ganga-Ma. The Mother. We would just sit and dream. He wanted to go to Los Angeles. Can you believe it? L.A. There he was, in the heart of purity, and he wanted modern big city action."

"And what did you want?"

"I just wanted peace."

"You hadn't found it yet?"

"I'd found an angel, or a couple of angels. I'd found an ashram. I'd found a wise old yogi. I'd found a path. But I hadn't found peace. Not yet."

"Well, what did you do?"

"Everything Swamiji said. All the asanas—the exercises, *dhyana*—the meditation, *japa*—the repetition of mantras, and pranayama—the breathing techniques. Reading the *Bhagavad Gita*, the *Upanishads*, the *Vedas*. Proper diet, proper breathing, proper relaxation, proper exercise, proper thinking and meditation. Everything! Swami Sivananda's program and teaching as continued through his disciples Swami Chidananda and my guy, Swami Krishnananda. And it was terrific. The discipline was just what I needed. We did work around the ashram. I watered plants, I planted plants, I did laundry, dishes, I cleaned up. Hell, I even cooked. And I'm a pretty good cook now. Make a mean *gobhi aloo* . . . that's cauliflower and potatoes in a nice spicy sauce. Cook some *basmati* rice, make some garlic *naan*, cucumber *raita*, you've got yourself a good meal."

I had to smile. The overindulged rock star/Snake Man that I knew had become a self-sufficient adult. A free man on the planet. "So it was your turn to learn how to do things instead of having things done for you," I said.

"And how to do things for others, too. That's the point of what I'm telling you. Service to others. Be of help, and support, and comfort to your fellow human beings. And guess what? It feels good. You begin to lose the grasping, greedy gimmies. It's no longer just me, me, me! It's about others, too. It's what Jesus was talking about two thousand years ago when he said, 'Love thy neighbor as thyself.' And when you're in a group of people who are giving . . . man, it becomes sweet. The energy becomes totally supportive. You feel so good, you begin to think *anything* is possible. Even world peace."

He laughed. "What an old '60s concept, huh? 'World Peace!' Why, you'd think I was a throwback to some archaic time. Not at all a postmodern guy. But I'll tell you, Roy, it's all possible. A new Garden of Eden is possible. With us, humanity, as the caretakers. We could create it in an instant. And that instant is called enlightenment. The yogis call it samadhi. All we have to do is open up to the beauty of the world. To break out of our shells, our egos. To go beyond the you and the me. To get outside of ourselves; to give up our childish fears and grasping and anger at not getting what we want. I certainly had to give up my rage, and my anger."

"Anger at what?" I asked the poet.

"At nothing, really. It's all so petty. Our petty egos can't control a particular situation so we get angry at whoever is around. We want others to do it our way, especially those who are close to us and those we love, and if they don't, we get angry and that turns into rage. In the big cities, and now the small towns of America, that rage turns into murder. People are actually killing each other because of their petty egos.

"But I'm telling you, it could be different. The earth, and all life, responds to positive energy. If we feel good, everything around us feeds off that feeling. If we feel happy, happy to be alive, we give off an energy that's good for all living things. And if groups of us begin to give off that kind of positive energy, the healing and growing increases one hundred–fold. We can begin to heal and transform everything on this planet with our positive energy. And do you know what that energy is called, Roy? It's simply called love."

I slapped him on the back. Now it was my turn to be excited. His energy was so reassuring I felt that anything was possible. "This is why you went on that journey," I said. "We'll make the music, you make the words. And just maybe we can play a little part in helping to save this planet. Are you with me?"

"I'm there, man. As much as I hate to leave my little tropical paradise, if we can play any part in the healing, I'm there."

I wrapped my arms around my old friend and squeezed him to me. There, beneath the Buddha tree, in the city of Victoria, on the island of Mahé, in the Seychelle Islands, in the middle of the Indian Ocean, due east of Mombassa. I hugged that old reprobate and he hugged me back. And I felt the sun radiating out of him, out of his heart center, and I knew everything could be as he said.

"If we're going to make music together, we've got some serious work to do, Roy. Are you sure you're up to it?"

I laughed. "Man, I've been waiting to hear you say this for twenty-five years. You're damn right I'm up to it! Are you?"

"Hey, I'm in pretty good shape for a former wreck. All I have to do is drop ten pounds and get my wind back. Do some hard swimming."

"And that cough," I said. "You've got to get rid of that cough. I don't like the sound of it."

He stopped for a second and thought. "You know," he said, "I haven't coughed since we left the Bar Gauguin. Must be something about the excitement of making plans, and talking about the future."

"Good. Because when you start to tell the stories of the ashram to the people—and your, what'd you call it? . . . your samadhi?—they're going to love it."

"Hold it, Roy. You're getting ahead of yourself. I never said anything about my samadhi and the ashram. Did I?"

"Well, no. Not exactly. I just assumed . . . "

"That can get you in trouble, my friend. Assumptions can be very misleading. And they're usually wrong."

I was confused. "But didn't you have a breakthrough at the ashram? All that discipline, that meditation. Didn't you find the answers?"

"No. I found discipline, joy, health, friendship, strength, dedication, beauty, and love at the ashram . . . but I didn't find me."

I stared at the Poet, confused. "Did you ever find you?"

"Of course. But not then. Do you remember why I said I went to India?"

"The feeling in the ocean. You wanted to recapture it."

"That was my quest. I stayed at the ashram for, I don't know, almost two years. I strained and struggled, grunted and sweated, and it just wouldn't come. And then one day I was out on a walk, a long walk up in the hills, in the beautifully forested hillsides leading up, eventually, to the great snow-covered peaks of the Himalayas. The source of Ganga-Ma. And sort of in the middle of nowhere I came across a series of caves in the hillside. They seemed to be roughly furnished. A little cloth and wood, mats and bedding, like someone was living in them. And then I saw that each cave had a little shrine set up. With candles, flowers, incense, and a picture of an Indian god, maybe Ganesh the elephant-boy god, who is the son of Shiva. Or maybe Shiva himself in contemplation, and a little stone *Shiva-linga*. Or Vishnu as the blue god. Or Hanuman, the monkey king."

"Vishnu and the hoodoo with the Sadhus," I rhythmically chanted, recalling his earlier stories.

"Yeah, there they were, in those caves. Sadhus, or actually apprentices, and one in particular. The leader of these ascetics was a Swami Shankardas. He was a younger guy, about our age. And I saw him sitting in his cave making a little tea. A nice chai tea that the Indians all love so much. I didn't know he was the guru at that moment, but he sure looked the part. Long dread-locks, loincloth, some jewelry around his neck, a few pieces of colorful cloth draped over his shoulders, and that was about it. Except for the look in his eyes. Those eyes said everything I wanted to know. Those eyes were the reason I came to India. He had seen the vision. He knew the secrets. He had the answer for me. I knew it. I could feel it. My senses were tingling. My skin had pulled itself up from my muscles and receiving a slight electrical charge. My arm hairs were waving like reeds in a breeze, and my neck hairs were on end. I had to go in to meet him.

"Before I could speak, he looked up and said, 'Come in. Would you like some chai?' I did a bow to him and said, 'Yes, *Baba*. Thank you.' He seemed to like that. 'How polite for an American.' He spoke English with a delightful lilt. 'You are an American, aren't you? You don't talk like, well, you don't even look like . . . an Englishman.' 'I'm from California, Baba,' I said. He smiled, 'Ahh, California. The Golden Land. Are you golden?' I didn't know what he meant. 'I don't think so. I don't really understand . . .' 'Then did you bring me anything golden?' he asked. 'No, Baba. I didn't even know you were here,' I said. He smiled, 'But here you are, aren't you? So you must know something.' 'I know my asanas, my postures,' I said. 'I know how to meditate. I do japa. I do pranayama, my breathing.' He clapped his hands together with delight. 'Wonderful!' he said. 'That's the hard part. Now sit down, have some tea, and let's see if we can make you gold.'

"He poured two cups of chai, sipped at his, and said: 'Let's just see if the lead that you are can be transformed into gold. I'll bet it can. You're in the alembic already. You are burning now, and it is only a short time longer until the alchemical transformation takes place. I can see it in your eyes. Why, you have even stopped your drinking, haven't you?' I was shocked. How did he know? I lowered my eyes. 'Yes, Baba, I have,' I said. He laughed. 'No need to be ashamed. So you were a drinker. So what? Now you are in the holy fire. Now you are being cleansed by the fire of *Agni*. And soon you will *truly* be from California. Golden.'

"The guy was a holy man, living in a makeshift cave above Rishikesh, and yet he was hip to all kinds of Western things. From alchemy to movies to rock and roll. He liked the Beatles 'All You Need Is Love.' Like my little angel in the street, he dug rock and roll. 'They have the right idea, those Beatles,' he said. I told him about our music. He said, 'See, *Devi* was with you and you were being consumed by Agni even back then.' This was all later of course. But right then as we sipped our tea, sitting on a mat, incense burning, Shiva the contemplative smiling down at us, I felt so very warmed and at peace. I felt like I could just sit there for a thousand years. We were surrounded by nothing except beauty. And we sat in silence, enjoying our chai.

"'What do you want to know, my friend?' *Swami-ji* finally said. 'I want to know who I really am,' I said. 'I had an experience in the ocean in which I seemed to leave my body, my self. It was blissful. So comforting. I want to, no, I must have it again.

And I want to know what I'm doing here, where I came from, where I'm going. I want to know where I was before I was born and what I'll be after I die. I want to know everything! But most of all I want to know who I am.' My heart was racing, the words came pouring out of me as if we were in the middle of a set in Madison Square Garden. I wanted to tell him everything in one long rush of free association. I felt like he was my Freudian/ Jungian/father, confessor/guru/psychiatrist all rolled into one cave-dwelling ascetic.

"'Catch your breath, my friend,' he said. 'Sip your tea. We have all the time in the world. And that's no time at all. Now just sip your tea. Enjoy the flavor. Feel the liquid washing over your tongue, going down your throat, through your chest, past your lungs, settling into your stomach, warming it. Relax my friend. Just relax.' His words were so soothing and hypnotic that my heart rate eased down to a slow blues tempo. My blood stopped rushing around in my brainpan. I took a deep breath, and sipped my tea. And Roy, that chai was absolutely delicious. I looked at Swami-ji and said, 'Baba, this is the best tea I've ever had. You are a master tea-brewer.' He smiled at me, like light, like Surya the Sun. "That's because you are drinking yourself, my friend."'

"I had no idea what he was talking about," the Poet said. "Talk about a Zen koan. How could I be drinking myself? And that's exactly what I asked him. 'Myself? How can I be . . . ' He didn't let me finish. 'You are the tea. Don't you want to know who you are?' he said. I nodded, suddenly sort of speechless. 'In India, we say *Tat Tvam Asi*. It means 'You are That.' What the tea is . . . you are. And the tea, my friend, is God.'

"I sat there in silence, contemplating those words. I sipped the tea again and looked at him. 'Then I am God?' He smiled, glowing again, radiating a heat and a subtle light. 'The nectar of

Brahman is that tea,' he said. 'And you are that tea. Therefore you are the nectar of Brahman. Your self is the all. Your *Atman*, your true self, is God. Brahman.'

"And then we sat there in silence. Not another word was said for a brief eternity. And in the ether an angel passed over our heads. I felt a strange opening in my heart. I felt chains beginning to fall away, chains that had bound my heart for my entire life. No, not my entire life. The chains weren't there when I was a child. The chains came later, as I matured. The warmth of that chai tea, was dissolving those chains that had bound my heart for so many years. And Roy, I began to feel like a child again! I began to feel a lightness in my solar plexus, in my rib cage. A sweet lightness that made me feel as if I were aloft, floating. A great warmth filled my being. I felt secure and radiant and warm and light as a feather. I felt giddy, almost silly, as if I was being tickled from the inside out.

"Then Baba spoke and the angel passed on. 'When you leave this cave, my friend,' he said, 'you will begin to see that *everything* is you, and you are everything. It is all one. You will begin to see—even better, you will begin to feel. Even as you are now. Tell me what you are feeling.'

"I said, 'I feel like a child again, Baba. Like a child!' Of course, he knew. He could sense it. 'Go out into the world, my friend. Walk in the trees of the forest and be your new self. Walk down to the river. Sit there . . . and be God. Go now. And come back to see me some time and tell me who you have been . . . and tell me who you are.'

"I kissed his hand, this holy man. 'Thank you, Baba,' I said. I bowed to him and went out into the amazingly intense green of that north Indian forest. And man, I felt good. I felt light and vigorous. I felt alive. For the first time in my life I realized I was actually alive! And the life around me was just vibrating. The energy coming off those plants was almost tangible. The trees and grasses and shrubs were throbbing with life. And the green . . . the color green! Such vibrancy everywhere around me. I raced down that hill, almost flying. It was an effortless run down to the river. I was in the zone. But so was everything else around me. We, the plants and I, were all in the zone. And guess what? We always are. All we have to do is feel it! It's always there. We're just not always there. Brahman is always there, waiting for us to remember who we are.

"And then I saw the river," the Poet continued. "I saw Ganga-Ma. I almost floated down to her. And when I got to her banks I took a great, deep breath and filled my lungs with the sweet, pure air of the Himalayas, the forest and Mother Ganges. And my heart chakra just burst wide open! The sweet air in my lungs broke those chains that had begun to dissolve because of the warmth of Swami Shakarda's chai. I was filled with freedom, with joy, with *energy*. Roy, it's all around us. It's always all around us. It *is* us! The divine energy is us, and *in* us, and in *everything*. It *is* everything. *We* are everything. And everything is God.

"And then, being so overwhelmed with that feeling I had to sit down, I found a little shade, under an acacia tree, and plopped down, resting my back against its trunk. And then I just stared at the river. At Ganga-Ma, and the light reflecting off of her. The dancing, dazzling light of Surya, the sun, reflecting off of Ganga-Ma.

"And I went into that light. I left everything behind, and I merged with the light. And in that instant I knew I was the light. I found the real me. I found who I really was. I was the light, and the light was God. The energy of the sun, the light, was the light of God. And I . . . was God."

Then the Poet stopped. He came to a rest and tilted his head up to the sun again and let the rays fall on his face. He smiled to himself. At peace with himself. The Poet, my friend, had truly been reborn.

"I had recaptured that feeling, Roy. I was in the ocean again, immersed in the ocean of bliss. And I floated on it. In a rapture. And then I dove in again. Except this time I dove into the light. I was absorbed by the gleaming light of Ganga-Ma. I realized that the waters of the Indian Ocean and the flowing Ganges were one and the same thing. And so was I! 'Tat Tvam Asi.' I was that. I had merged with the energy. And *that* is the divine secret. God is the energy. We are the energy. Ergo, we are God. As Jesus said, 'I and the Father are One.'"

He grew silent again, and then he looked at me with a great softness in his eyes, a great warmth. And I imagined that the look of the yogi in the cave and the look of the Poet were one and the same.

"I had come home to myself," he said. "My exile was finally over."

13

I went back to the ashram late that evening, after watching the sun set and seeing the light change through the entire spectrum of colors. The glow of Surya slowly disappeared, everything went softly dark, and then came the moonlight—that opalescent orb. Its light was cooling and soothing. That pale silver light dancing off the Ganges was enthralling. I sat late into the evening, feeling blessed and divine and one. The veil had been lifted. I was no longer ensnared in the web of Maya. I had broken through. I was now on the other side. Forever.

"Finally, I drifted back to the ashram. I don't even remember how. I certainly don't remember walking."

He laughed to himself.

"Perhaps I floated back. In that state of bliss anything seems possible. And when I walked through the little saffron gate and passed the pillar of rules in the central courtyard, there was Swami Krishnananda, sitting in a chair and gazing up at the full moon. He heard me, looked over and said 'Come, my son, sit with me. Let us watch our mother in the sky together.' I went to him and sat by his side. He put his hand on my shoulder, like a father, looked into my eyes . . . and smiled. 'You know now, don't you,' he said. 'You have found the answer. You know who you really are.' 'Yes, Father,' I said. I pointed at the moon. 'I am that.' And he laughed with the sound of bells, light and free. 'I am so happy for you, my son. Doesn't it feel good? Don't you feel alive? For the first time in your life don't you feel truly alive?' He knew everything. He could read me like a book. 'Yes, Father,' I said, 'I feel so alive. I am everything and everything is me. I am the light of the sun reflecting off our mother, the moon. How beautiful she is tonight. How luminous.'

"He smiled at me. 'And are you also the rabbit in the moon?' And that stumped me. He could always do that, the wise old man. 'What rabbit?' I asked. 'In the moon. Don't you see it?' 'I see the man in the moon.' Evidently, he found that very funny. He giggled. 'No, no, no. Don't look with Western eyes, look with Eastern eyes. The rabbit is sideways. Two ears, a head, the body in profile. The man is looking straight at us. The rabbit is looking up. See?'

"I stared at the moon for I don't know how long. I was the light of the moon. I kept drifting into the pale silver, but I'll be damned if I could see the rabbit. 'He is the lucky rabbit,' *Yogiji* said. 'Once you see him, you will always have good fortune. Of course, now that you know who you really are . . . you will have no need for good fortune. You *are* fortune.'

"Then I saw it. Like Don Juan told Carlos Castaneda, I shifted my vision, and there it was! The lucky rabbit. 'I see it, Father. He's facing upwards. Two ears, a head, his body in profile. I see the rabbit in the moon.'

"'Very good, my son. Now, I truly have nothing left to teach you,' he said, laughing again. And his laughter was so contagious I had to join him. We sat there, filled with delight and laughing into the night air, into the starry sky, into the vault of heaven—two rabbits in the moon.

"Then we fell into a deep silence. We sat together, two men, alive on the planet. In love with the planet, with the all. I felt his energy merge with mine, and our collective energy merge with the soft, night air that was perfumed with flowers and glowing with an opalescent light. And I lost the fear. All my fears were gone, dissolved into memory that was then dissolved into the ether, never to be a concern of mine again. I had no reason to fear anything because there was no anything. There was only everything. And I was everything. And I, or rather we, the Swami and I, were God. There was no differentiation, hence there was nothing to fear.

"Roy, I lost all resentment at that moment. I didn't begrudge my father anything, anymore. All the childhood slights—the lack of warmth from my mother, the long absences of my father, the various humiliations and traumas at school, the bullies, the failures with girls—just disappeared. I didn't care anymore. It was the greatest therapeutic session one could ever have. Beyond anything that Sigmund Freud could have imagined. I was released, unblocked. Bam! All at once, just like that. And all those childhood traumas, I later realized, were just tempering the steel. Those terrible slights are what eventually cause us to say 'Why am I alive? What's the purpose of existence?' And ultimately, bottom-line, 'Why aren't I happy?' Asking those questions puts you on the path. Because we are all in exile. In exile from our true selves."

He looked at me deeply, with a great warmth in his eyes. "But Roy, we are one! We are all one. And—heresy of heresies, abomination and blasphemy—we are all God. And the potential to know that is in all of us. It's the journey we are all on. The journey to self-realization. My self is the all-self. All our selves are the all-self.

"And man, if I can realize that, so can anybody. If this Snake Man, degenerate, egocentric, greedy, evil, boorish bastard asshole that you're talking to right now can merge into the oneness . . . then so can anybody!"

I was so blown away by the Poet's revelations that I felt I had to return his attention to mundane detail. "So how much longer did you stay in India? After your samadhi?"

"That very evening Swami Krishnananda said to me, 'You can leave now, my son. Or you can stay with us and perfect your experience. I am here to help you in any way I can, although you no longer have any need of me.' And I replied, 'I would like to stay a while longer, Father. I need to relate this experience to my life, to all life. To why we do what we do to each other. To the killing and the suffering, the angst and the malaise. To the why of the world.' And then I looked at my wise old teacher, 'And I still don't have some of the asanas down. Father, I can't do the Wheel. I can't raise my body up off the floor. I can stay with my hands, head and feet touching the floor, but I can't extend my body up into the arch.'

"And Swamiji laughed, 'My son, it took me two years to perfect *Chakrasana*. That posture is very difficult. Stay with us, then, until you think out the relationships of the world, or until you perfect Chakrasana. Then I want you to go into the world and live your life. Your new life. For now you are the new man. Now you remember who you are. Now you are the infinite.'

"So I stayed for another six months or so, and finally mastered the wheel. That was one tough asana, but I got strong enough to do it. It was all in the arms. I was just one weak-armed writer boy from the States. But they finally got strong enough to support my body in that upside-down, hands and feet on the floor, arms and legs fully extended, navel pointing up at the blue sky posture."

"That sounds tough," I said.

"Someday I'll teach it to you," he said. "It really opens up the chest. You'll like it, and you should be able to do it. You've got those big arms. Hell, we'll do it together. I'll teach you my little *Hatha* yoga routine."

"I'd like that," I said. "We can do it together."

"*Ha* is the breath of the sun, *tha* is the breath of the moon. *Prana* is the in-breath, the taking in of the energy—the *chi*, as the Chinese call it. Prana is the breath of life that permeates and sustains everything. *Apana* is the out-breath, the expelling of waste, the cleansing breath. Hatha yoga is the uniting of these breaths, the uniting of the sun and the moon."

"More songs," I said. "The 'Breath of the Sun' is a great title. And the uniting of the sun and the moon. Like a wedding, an alchemical wedding . . . a heavenly wedding. A great *love* song."

"'A Love Supreme,' huh?" the Poet said. "Like John Coltrane. He was a giant, an enlightened one. It's too bad he had to be taken from us so young."

"That's what we used to say about you. 'Too young.'"

"Well, I'm not dead and don't plan to be for a long time. And here we are today, just like on the beach at El Segundo—as the Hawaiians say . . . talking story."

"And planning a future," I added. "Except this time around it'll be a lot more fun for you. This time around it's music for healing."

"Music for transport," the Poet said. "Music for the soul. But with all the drama of the eternal struggle intact. We've got to keep the terror in the music, Roy."

"Hey," I said. You're talking to the Slavic iceman. We're not talking background music here. We're talking passion—the nightmare of the soul and its final triumph."

"Right!" he said. "I want passion above everything else. Today we lack the drive towards transcendence. Hell, we don't even know about the *possibilities* of transcendence. We think this is the final point. I read a Jesuit tract that said we, mankind, are at the conclusion in our evolutionary relationship to God. In other words, he's above, we're below, and we will be united with God after death. Well sweet jumping Jesus, is the point of our life to die? I don't think so. The point is to live! To live in the light of love and understanding. In the merging of our individual soul with the all-soul. 'I and the Father are one,' Yesuha ben Joseph said."

"You are that," I said. "Isn't that what the yogi in the cave said? Aren't those the words that opened you up as you sipped his tea? As you sipped yourself?"

The Poet laughed, delighted. "You've got it, amigo. I drank that tea . . . and that tea was me. And I owe all thanks, all honor, and all blessing to Swami Shankardas. He brought me out of the prison of myself. He unlocked the chains around my heart, the chains of my own ego, and I was able to come out of exile! Into freedom, Roy. Into freedom!"

"Did you ever see him again?"

"Oh yes. That's why I stayed at the ashram another six months. I went to see Swami Shankardas almost every day. We'd talk, and he'd serve his chai of Brahman."

"What did you talk about?"

"Things I want to sing about. Write poems about. Tell the world about."

He closed his eyes, took a deep breath, held it for a long time, and slowly began to expel it. And the hissing came again, the almost reptilian sound from somewhere inside his throat as the air passed out of his nostrils. When his lungs were empty, cleansed, he rested in that emptiness for a moment, took another deep breath, and began to speak:

"We've got to do our small part in setting up some healing rhythms, some deep, throbbing rhythms that hit people low in the chest. And I want to float stories over the top of those rhythms. Stories from the beginning. Maybe dramatize Adam and Eve, for instance."

A mischievous grin crept across his face. "You know the fable: God shouts down from above after Adam has eaten the apple. 'Hey, Adam! You little dirt bag! I told you not to eat the apple . . . and you did! What is the matter with you, are you nuts? Are you *meshugenah*?!' God speaks Yiddish, you know."

I laughed. "See, I didn't know that."

"Oh yeah, it's a little-known fact, but he does," the Poet said, his eyes alight. "So, God's really angry. Adam has disobeyed the big guy, and God doesn't like to be disobeyed. He likes to be worshipped. In fact, he has a circle of angels—the seraphim—surrounding him at the highest level and all they do is gaze upon God and say 'Holy, Holy, Holy.' And he likes that. He offered Lucifer—some say his most beautiful creation—a chance to be in that upper echelon of spiritual beings, sort of the inner circle, and Lucifer said, 'No! I'm not going to worship you. I'm your equal. I'm as good as you, why should I worship you?'

"And God was furious, just like with Adam. He said to

Lucifer, 'You got one last chance, boy. You worship me, or I'll send you to . . . uhh . . . to, I swear I'll send you to . . . ' See, God hadn't created hell yet. None of the angels had sinned. Lucifer was the first sinner. And then God hit upon an idea. 'Eternal damnation!' he said. 'I'll send you to *Hell*, boy! You'll suffer for all eternity. You'll never see me again, ever!' And Lucifer said, 'But you created me. Why should you damn me?' And God said 'Because you're arrogant! You've committed the first transgression against God. The sin of pride. You think you're as good as me! And you're not! So . . . go to Hell! And that was it. Poof! Lucifer and all his followers—evidently there were quite a few who didn't want to worship God in that way, standing around him in a circle going 'Holy, Holy, Holy,' evidently they thought they *were* God so why should they worship Him? It would be like worshipping themselves, and that would be unseemly. Some bizarre kind of self love. So they refused . . . and poof! They were all thrown into Hell in the blink of an eye. And there they remain to this very day. Thinking they're as good as God. The sin of pride, Roy. The sin of pride."

"And this is a true story?" I asked.

"Absolutely. You don't think I made up this tale, do you? This is Christian tradition. This is bedrock."

"And so is Adam and Eve," I said.

"That's right, that's the story I was going to tell. We are the descendants of Adam. We are his children. And here's the kind of guy he was, our progenitor.

"So God is hollering at Adam, 'You piece of filth! You little shit! You *putz*! I told you not to do it and you did it. Why? You better have a good answer, Adam. Why did you eat the apple?'

"And Adam, knees knocking and almost ready to wet his fig leaf, is trying to figure some way of escaping God's wrath. So he tries to shift the blame, being just the way we are today, and says: 'It's not my fault. *She* made me do it!'

"This little coward points at his woman. At Eve. And tries to dump the blame on her. Instead of standing up to God and saying 'Okay, I ate the apple. Big deal. So what? I'm to blame. I take full responsibility.' Does he do that? Does he act like a man? Does he look God square in the eye and say 'I'm responsible? Hell, no! The coward blames his wife. The beautiful, sensuous, loving Eve. His helpmate, his other half, his rib. He blames her. *She made me do it!*' And God throws them, and therefore all of us, into exile. What a pathetic ending to the Garden of Eden.

"And that's the official Bible story. Western civilization is based on that story. Judaism, Christianity, and Islam are all based on that story. We are all descended from Adam—and he didn't even have the *cojones* to take the blame. And today, consequently, the last thing in the world we want to do is to be responsible. And Roy, the *first* thing we have to do is assume responsibility. And I mean for everything! We are responsible for the whole planet and everything on it. It's ours. We made it up. We are the creator. We are the mind of God. We *are* God. This is our creation. And damn it, we better love it, because it's all we've got! This is it—there ain't no more."

I was overwhelmed . . . and laughing. "You're not suggesting a rewrite of the Bible, are you?"

"No, man, we're just gonna make 'em think about it in, you know, mythological terms. People just have to see it as a grand story, full of psychological needs and projections. Very big on authority figures—a real daddy problem. And lots of weird spooky stuff that kids like. For instance, that last book of the New Testament, the Apocalypse, *Revelations*. What a fright-show that is. A horrible tale of the end times and the loathsome beast 666. Who let that in the Bible in the first place? It's a fuck-ing nightmare. People are getting the bejesus scared out of them; good, decent Christian men and women are terrified. They're in a psychological panic. They've got the fear, big-time. They can't love this good, green earth. They can't embrace the beauty of life, the joy of life. They're only concerned about the *end* of life. And internally, their nerve ends are shattered by the horror of this paranoid tale. This Apocalypse, this Book of Revelations."

"They believe every word of it," I said.

"I know. And guess what, it ain't so! It's not the Word. Because the Word is *love*. And the word 'love' is not in that last book of the New Testament. The end times are not coming. The earth will continue to revolve around the sun for millions and millions of years. Life on this miraculous planet will continue to exist for untold millennia until the sun eventually loses its heat. Until Surya gradually grows cooler and cooler and finally gives up all its life-sustaining energy. Then, and only then, will we, the living, come to an end on Mother Earth.

"And there won't be any parting of the heavens, either—with Jesus coming back on a white charger accompanied by a host of angels. The sky can't part. There's nothing behind it. It's infinite. Besides, there's no need for Jesus to come back a second time. He was already here. Did you miss it? Well, he left his message. Have you heard it? More importantly, are you living it? And do you even know what it is? Well it's love! Love the lord, thy God, and love thy neighbor as thy self. The Atman, your true inner self is the Brahma—the all. Your self is your neighbor is God. That's the message of Jesus and the Buddha, and *all* the religions of the world. There's no need for him to come again; he said it all the first time."

"We are the supreme act of love."

"Exactly. The love supreme."

And the melody of John Coltrane's ode to love began singing in my brain. I could hear Elvin Jones's drums, and McCoy Tyner's piano, and Jimmy Garrison's bass, all locking together with Coltrane's tenor sax and the mantra "A Love Supreme, a Love Supreme" rolling over and over itself in my mind's ear. They were all one. The musicians had entered that sacred space where all egos were dissolved and only the rhythm and the chord changes and the melody and that mantra "A Love Supreme" existed. It was a state that we had often entered in our rock-band days. And as I listened to the John Coltrane quartet playing in my head I knew that we, the Poet and I and the drummer and the guitar player, could enter that state again. We could be one with the music again. One with each other again. The Poet was alive, and we were going to do it one more time. One more divine and glorious time.

My eyes began to fill with tears of joy, and my joy spilled down my cheeks.

"You're tripping, man," the Poet said. "What's going on in that brain of yours?"

I sniffled and laughed. "I'm having a flashback," I said. "I'm digging on Coltrane doing 'A Love Supreme,' and I'm seeing us on stage at the Irish Mist. We're all together —and I'm having a flash-forward, too. We're on stage again, and you're singing, and the three of us are supporting you, and you're telling stories of the divine . . . and, man . . . I love it! I can't even contain it, I feel so good. I can't tell you what it means to me that you're alive."

"You told me, amigo. You don't need words for that."

The Poet stretched himself in the dappled shade of the great Buddha tree, in the central square of the city of Victoria, on the island of Mahé, in the Seychelles, in the middle of the Indian Ocean, some 1,500 miles due east of Mombassa on the African coast.

"Now it's time to meet my family," he said. "Besides, I'm getting hungry. Angelique will have one of her great stews going and the kids are gonna want to meet you. Dad's old college friend who's come all the way from California."

He rose from the bench. I wiped the joy from my eyes, stood up alongside him, and we moved off. Into the light.

14

The softness was all around me as we moved through the town. I seemed to be enveloped by a warmth beyond physical heat. It was, if anything, a spiritual heat. A light seeming to emanate from the earth itself.

"Do you feel like I do?" I asked the Poet. "The energy of this place? I feel so . . . safe here."

"A benevolence," the Poet said. "You can feel it here more than any place I've ever been. That's why I came back after I left India. Where was I going to go? This is the Garden of Eden. So I came back to the garden. My exile was over. The expulsion was over. The gates were reopened, and the angels with the fiery swords who were guarding the gates had been dismissed, their duty completed. So I walked right in to reclaim my garden. And this time I wasn't going to blame Eve. That is, if I could find her."

"And did you?" I asked.

"We're going home to dinner, aren't we?" the Poet responded.

We continued through the softness. The lush green of the island and the sea-swept, perfumed air enfolded us. Heavy tropical blooms floated their intoxicating scents into the twilight time that was now approaching. The sun was beginning to dip and the birds of the Seychelles were starting their end-of-day concerto. Contrapuntal melodies competed for space in the aural spectrum, flitting about with a divine grace and delicacy. They performed call and response in a scale known only to them, but a scale of such sweetness that I was enraptured.

"How beautiful it is here, my friend," I said to the Poet. "No wonder you returned."

He smiled. "It's especially fine at this time of day. The approach of sunset brings out a special quality in the air. It seems to soften. And so does the light."

"And to listen to those birds," I added. "That song is so beautiful. Such controlled cacaphony, I love it."

The Poet listened for a moment. "Perhaps you could write some music to approximate this beauty. You know, like when you played rain on our song about the thunderstorm in Joshua Tree. Only this time, instead of being all dark and moody, you could play as light as a feather. Make people hear what you're hearing now, and maybe feel a bit of what you're feeling now. They'd love to feel that intoxication, that warmth. That's what music is supposed to do, isn't it?"

"Absolutely," I said. "I'll try to capture the song of the birds if you'll write a poem to their thoughts. You tell us what they're thinking and I'll play what they're feeling. What do you say, shall we try it?"

"Whoa, man. That's a big order. What the birds are thinking?"

"Why not?" I said. "This is your garden. You are those birds. You can find their thoughts in you. Can their joy be any different than ours? Right here, right now, aren't we all feeling the same softness?"

"We certainly are," the Poet said. "After all, we're the same energy. We came from the same source and we're occupying the same space at the same time. Our souls and their souls are exactly the same, so why shouldn't we all be feeling the same thing? I think I'll give it a try, Roy. Yes, I believe I will."

"The light is almost gone," I said. "Sun's fading."

The Poet put his hand out as if he were feeling the energy in the dimming light, cupping it softly, like a woman's breast.

"The light may be fading," he said, "but God is always there, waiting for us to come to our senses. The energy is always there. All we have to do is open ourselves to it. To just feel it. One touch, and our exile is over. One touch and we're free men and women, alive on planet Earth. Spinning around the sun. Racing through the universe. Reborn in the light, amigo."

We walked along in silence. The Poet's words hung in the air. There was nothing left to say. I was with him, and we were simply alive in the moment.

We had left the town of Victoria and were now on a small road weaving through the lush vegetation, enveloped by the green. And then the darkness descended. The birds' song of twilight was finished. The sun was finished for the day. It was now the moon's turn to illuminate the land. A pale, milky light barely showed us the road as we moved on to our dinner date at the Poet's house somewhere in the middle of this now pearlescent green. I followed him in a speechless delight. The heat had begun to abate. A muted bouquet enveloped us as the perfume of the night flowers began its sweet task of intoxication. It was the night of the Garden of Eden. I was ecstatic with the moment, and with the enormous possibilities of our future. And before I could speak, he said, "Here we are."

We turned off the road onto a small path, and the green became pitch black, and the black was in our faces. It was thick, dense, and vaguely foreboding. Had I not been with the Poet, I would have begun to feel a sense of threat. All that vegetation was more than most city dwellers can handle. I began to feel at the mercy of outside forces. Forces beyond the parameters of my usual existence. Primeval powers, which had conjured this globe and maintained its revolution.

I began to feel inconsequential in that deep black. It was as if I didn't matter. "It's so incredibly dark here," I said to the Poet. "It's as if all light has been turned off permanently. I feel completely unconnected."

The Poet laughed. "That happened to me too. It took the longest time for me to get used to the change from day into night. The days are so brilliant and then night falls like the proverbial final curtain. Blackout, right? And you feel lost in it."

"That's how I feel right now," I said. "And completely unnecessary, too."

"You got it, man. We *are* unnecessary. Our presence is not necessary for the continuation of this good, green world. Nature is here with or without us, the energies are here in their own place and time. They don't need us. They simply continue their work of reproducing life and maintaining the planet.

"You see, Roy, it's all a projection from deep inside of us. We don't understand the power, the energy of maintenance—what has been called the telluric force. We're out of harmony with our own creation, and so we think the energy is something outside of us. We can sense it, but we don't know what it is, and so we create a spirit world to answer our questions about the unseen, but deeply felt, power of the planet. Of all existence, for that matter. And since we're afraid and unsure of our place in that existence, we have created an unnecessarily complex scenario of a battle between good and evil. An eternal battle until some last and final judgement casts everyone either into heaven or hell . . . forever. And until that judgement, our minds and fears create evil entities that populate our world with us.

"The devil doesn't exist, Roy. Only our minds exist, and we have personified our fears of the dark into demons that have no reality. It's all within us. And this blackness brings it out, doesn't it?"

"Yeah," I said. "It's so black I feel like a kid again. Unsure of myself."

"That's how most people feel all the time. They cover it with a veneer of sophistication, a patina of knowledge, but inside is the same terrified child, alone in the dark. But there's really nothing to fear."

He touched my arm and stopped us, there in that heart of darkness.

"Where did Jesus say the kingdom of heaven was?"

"Well," I said, trying but failing to remember my Bible lessons, "people think heaven is up in the clouds somewhere. Or beyond the clouds, in a spiritual place that's somehow . . . filled with clouds."

The Poet smiled. "Kind of silly, isn't it? That cloud place. The kingdom of heaven is within you! That's what Jesus said, and of course he was right."

The Poet placed his hand over his heart. Then he moved it from his heart onto my heart. And the warmth of his hand seemed to rush into me. Making me feel secure and alive in that darkness.

"It's all right here, Roy. The heart chakra."

Then a female voice called out of the darkness, "Joseph, is that you?"

"Yes, my love," the Poet responded back. "And I have some-one with me. Someone from a long time ago." He squeezed my arm. "A friend . . . a good friend."

"Well, bring him, then. The *callaloo* is ready." The voice was sweet and had a Creole song in it.

"That's my Angelique," the Poet said to me. "Come on."

He strode off into the darkness. I quickly fell in behind him, not wanting to get left behind in that huge blackness. We moved forward a dozen yards or so and there it was, his little house. A Victorian cottage from a hundred years ago with lights warming the windows, all cozy and inviting. And there *she* was, standing in the front yard, a lithe, lovely, café-au-lait Seychelloise, wearing an Indian-print dress with her hair in multiple braids. We came up to her and the Poet took her in his arms and kissed her deeply, full on the lips. And I saw more than passion in that kiss. I saw completion. It was only for an instant, but in that kiss the two of them seemed to merge into one another. The eternal separation, the eternal loss of our other half was found and completed in that embrace, in that kiss. And I realized how much they meant to each other, how much they needed each other.

"Darling, this is Roy," he said. "From the band . . . from America." Then he pinched her butt. "But you already know that, don't you."

"Ouch," she said laughingly as she swatted away his pinch. Then she took my hand. "You are welcome, mister Roy. My name is Angelique."

I was enthralled by her. By her beauty, the lilt in her voice, the warmth of her touch, the marvelous color of her skin and the compassion in her eyes. "I am so pleased to meet you, Angelique. Your husband and I knew each other many years ago."

"I know," she said. "You are the organ player. And you have hardly changed at all. How do you stay so young looking?"

"How nice of you to say that, Angelique. I only wish it were true," I said.

"But it *is* true," she said. And I heard island song-birds in her voice. "You look almost like you do in the photos I have of the band. You should grow your hair long again, however. Then people would think you had been in a time machine."

The three of us laughed together, and I felt at ease with them, there in their front yard, on the island of Mahé, in the Seychelles, in the middle of the Indian Ocean.

"So how do you do it?" she continued. "How do you stay so fit?"

"Well, I work out, I eat fresh and natural food, and I love my wife," I said.

The Poet chuckled. "Me, too. That's exactly what I do."

Angelique playfully slapped him on the arm. She was indeed full of spirit. "You do not work out."

"Well, maybe I don't," the Poet said. "But I do eat your good food. And I do love you." He grabbed her in a bear hug, lifted her off her feet and spun her around. She squealed with delight.

"Well, come on then," he said as he lowered his Angelique to the ground. "Let's get our feet under the dining table. I'm starved!"

We went inside and the colors of the interior were a reflection of their love for each other: bright, vibrant, alive and enthralling. Turquoise blues, lemon yellows, luxurious pinks—a rainbow of tropic warmth.

The table was set with plates that could have come directly from Monet's house in Giverny; they sat upon a red paisley Indian-print tablecloth. In the center a large bowl of greens was waiting to be dressed. A long baguette waited patiently next to the salad, its partner—a tub of butter—close by its side. The Poet took to the salad as Angelique went to the stove. He deftly drizzled a bottle of olive oil over the greens, splashed a red wine vinegar on top of that, hit the salad with sea salt and fresh ground pepper and tossed the whole with an ebony fork and spoon set. His movements were sure and easy.

At the stove, Angelique was ladling a beautiful fish stew into a large tureen shaped like a sea turtle. The stew was thick with island bounty—vegetables and seafood—luxuriating in a reddish-golden broth that smelled deliciously of curry and Creole Louisiana. As she ladled, Angelique called out to the children. "Michael, Louise! Dinner is ready. Please bring the wine and mineral water."

And out they came from their little rooms. The boy I had talked to on the street and his younger sister—and they were gorgeous. With curled ringlets of dark blonde hair, and a tawny, golden glow to their complexions. Their features were beyond racial classification. They were the new golden race. It is said that in the future the races will merge—black, white, brown, red, and yellow all coming together—and there will only be one race, the human race, and its color will be golden. If that is to be the case, then the Poet and his Angelique have already begun the process.

The children bounded into the kitchen, kissed their mother, ran over to the Poet and hugged him warmly.

"Kids," the Poet said, "this is my friend, Roy. He's from the United States. We knew each other a long time ago, in college."

"How do you do, Monsieur Roy," they said in unison, lilting English and French together. "I am Michael," the boy said. "We knew you were coming, that's why I spoke to you in town today." And he looked over at his mother and winked, conspiratorially.

"I am Louise," the girl said, as the island birds sang through her voice just as they did through her mother's. "We are happy to have you, Monsieur Roy. "Someday I will go to the United States. To New York City."

"It's very, very big, Louise," I said. "And it's not at all like Victoria. It's all concrete and crowded . . . "

"And full of life, yes?" she said.

"Well . . . yes. It is full of life," I replied.

"And that's why I want to go there."

"Take care of the water, Louise," the Poet said to her. "And open the wine, Michael."

"Yes, papa," Louise said. She nudged her brother and they jumped to their tasks.

"Your daughter looks like her mother but she has you inside of her," I said to the Poet.

He sighed, "Yes, she has the wanderlust and the gift of gab."

I laughed. "What about Michael?"

"Too soon to tell, but he swims like a fish."

"He has your balance. I saw him on his skateboard this morning."

"Leaping about like a monkey, no doubt."

"Yes, they were all sort of flying. He and his friends."

He sighed again. "They grow up so fast. The time flies by now. The pace here used to be so slow and now it races past me."

I protested, "But it's such a leisurely tempo here. A very lush bolero. Nothing's racing. What are you talking about?"

He touched my arm, gently. "I'm talking about my life, old friend."

And I saw a deep and profound compassion in his eyes. The adventures of the years had given him a view on life that the "snake man" never had. In his youth he was a wild and lustful indulger of all sensations. He could never be satisfied. He was always after more.

But now, he had turned himself around and become a lover of the world. And the world had taken on a fragile quality for him. A fleeting transience that he saw reflected in his own life. And it touched him deeply.

"How quickly life moves when you finally become aware of its sweetness," he said. "When we were young, the days were interminable. Today, twenty-four hours are not nearly enough. I need forty-eight hours in a day to do it justice, to give each moment its own fullness. It seems that every instant carries a weight and meaning that throws me back to that little cave in India, to the understanding I had in India. Roy, I want to dwell on each moment and consider its profundity but before I can, the next moment of infinity has come racing in for its dance on the stage. And I become overwhelmed with moments in time flying by me. And it's all so damned sweet . . . it makes me laugh. All of us doing our little dances on the stage of life and thinking it's so profound. And it's nothing but drops in the ocean. We're an eye-dropper filled with an elixir called life, and drop by drop we empty our containers into the sea. And the divine energy continually swirls and dances all around us, and all we have to do is open our eyes to see it. And then, man, it's ride-the-racehorse time. I can't believe how fast this roller-coaster ride is."

Then he laughed and slapped me on the back. "And I fucking love it!"

I had to smile, too. The Poet was so alive and vibrant, his family was so good to be with, his home was so warm and comfortable, that I felt surrounded by a glow of peace and security.

"God, I feel good," I said. It exploded out of me and I laughed at my outburst.

Angelique heard me from her post at the stove. "Well, I am happy you find our home and company so enjoyable, mister Roy."

"I do, Angelique. I certainly do."

"If you feel good now," the Poet said, "wait till you taste this *bourride*. Angelique whips up one of the best fish stews on the island. This is going to bring a fine smile to your belly." And he called out to her. "Honey, can you serve that magnificent turtle to us now? I can see he's just bursting with anticipation and excitement!"

"It's all ready, my love," she sang back. The majolica tureen floated to the table in Angelique's arms as Michael and Louise brought the water and wine. The crusty French bread was broken, the salad plates filled with crisp greens, the top was taken off the turtle and we all said, "Ahhh."

The feast began and we set to it in a hungry silence. I was completely enthralled with the simple yet deep flavors of that meal. Angelique had infused that humble fare with sophistication and a love that you could taste. She seemed so happy, so alive, and so in love with the Poet and their beautiful children. Our meal reflected that love and it was good to be at the Poet's table.

Then we were finished. In what seemed like the blink of an eye the meal was consumed and the plates were polished clean. The magnificent turtle stood empty, his work done for the day. The children popped up from their places, jabbered about a ballet class and meeting friends at the town square, and began to clear the table. They were lively kids but seemed to be well-disciplined. They had their little chores and performed them with grace and acceptance.

"You seem to have them well-trained," I whispered to the Poet.

"Oh, sure . . . for now. But puberty hasn't set in yet. Wait 'till those hormones start racing. Then we'll see about 'polite.' It'll go right out their sex glands."

"Joseph, please." Angelique said, sotto voce. "Not with the children around."

"They didn't hear anything, darling. Their heads are in the clouds. They really don't pay attention to what adults talk about."

Angelique grinned at him. "They do when we talk about sex." And her voice was so sultry that I immediately understood why the Poet was in love with her.

"You're right, as usual," he said. "I suppose I really ought to use the term 'second chakra' from now on."

"Exactly," Angelique said. "Put that Indian experience of yours to practical use."

The Poet laughed. "Darling, I try to do that every day."

She smiled at him. "I know you do. But you also know I have to tease you about it."

"Oh, saucy wench." I could see the Poet's love and desire for her flash in his eyes.

"Papa," Louise called from the sink where they had stacked the dishes and the turtle. "Can we go now?"

The Poet smiled at them, "Yes, of course. Go to your lessons and your friends."

They ran to their mother, kissed her on the cheek, said "*Adieu, Monsieur Roy,*" and bolted out the door.

"Hey!" the Poet called at them.

They came back to the doorway. "Yes, papa?"

"Don't forget . . . enjoy yourselves."

They laughed. "Yes, papa!" they said in unison, and were gone. Into the warm, tropic night. Into paradise.

"Can I make you a *café filtre*, mister Roy?" asked Angelique. "Or would you like some cheese and fruit for dessert? We have a nice Reblochon that just came in yesterday from Paris."

"Coffee will be more than enough, Angelique. That stew was exquisite and very filling," I said. "It's one of the nicest blending of flavors I've ever had."

She smiled. "Thank you, but it wouldn't be what it is without its brief rest in our turtle. He has a magic."

The Poet laughed. "Oh, yes. He is a direct descendant of the great turtle that supports the entire world . . . according to the Indian myth."

"I'd love to do music to that if you'll tell the story. 'The Earth Turtle.' Yes . . . a kind of music of support, don't cha' know."

"Are you mocking my Southernisms, Roy?" he laughed. "I don't sound like that, do I?"

"You certainly do, my love," Angelique responded. "You use those funny little phrases about swamps and 'gators and even hush puppies, half the time I don't know what you're talking about."

The Poet roared at that one. I had to laugh with him at the sheer delight he took in her as Angelique returned his laughter with bells of her own. And there we sat, in the Poet's house, laughing to the moon.

"Please, darling, some coffee," he said when his delight finally subsided. "And bring a little cognac with it. I'm going to indulge myself with brandy and a cigar. After all, it's not everyday one comes back from the dead . . . don't cha' know."

He started laughing again, but this time his cough reappeared, and the phlegm sounded deep in his lungs as the cough racked him twice.

"No cigar for you, Joseph," said Angelique. "You really shouldn't smoke them. Listen to you."

"I agree," I said. "You have to give up that smoking if you're ever going to get your voice back in shape. How the hell are you going to sing on stage with all that phlegm in your lungs?"

Angelique stared at me, the light slipping out of her eyes. "What do you mean 'sing on stage'?"

"We're going to do it again, Angelique," I said. We're going to create new songs, for the new time! Songs of, of . . . "

"Possibilities," the Poet said, completing my thought. "Nothing more than that, Roy. Just the possibilities of transformation."

"It'll be for everyone, Angelique!" I said. "For everyone who's looking for something to complete themselves. Everyone who's looking to end their own exile."

"Whoa, easy," the Poet protested. "We're not going to be doing all that. It's just going to be poetry and music. Nothing more than it was when we first started playing together. My point of view has changed, but I don't know if my poetic abilities are any better. I'll just be telling some stories. Just stringing some words together. The interpretation will be up to the listener. You and the drummer and the guitar player make the music. I'll make the words. But we're not saving souls here, amigo. This is not a mission. This is my version of, as Samuel Beckett said, How It Is. So don't be putting your overheated hype on what we're going to do. Just play it cool, boy . . . real cool. And that's how we're gonna do it—can you dig it?"

"I love it, man. *Real cool.* I can do that."

Angelique came out of her trance. "Do what?" she said. "What are you two scheming?"

"Now, love," the Poet said. "I was going to tell you, but Roy just blurted it out in his usual overly enthusiastic way and put it on the table without the proper presentation."

"No fancy words, please. I don't need a buildup. I can think for myself, Joseph. Just tell me what he meant by 'sing on stage.'"

"Well, my love, we're going to put the band together again. We're going to write some new songs, record them and then go on the road and perform them for the people."

"No, you can't!" she protested. And her eyes were filled with desperation and fear.

He took her hand. "Darling, I'm not going to leave you and the children and become that reprobate again. It'll only be for a short while. I have many poems that Roy and the guitar player could easily set to music. I won't be gone long. It'll all happen very quickly. I'm too old to be wasting my time now."

"So am I, Angelique," I said. "I'll take him away from you for as little time as possible. But we do have to go back to Los Angeles. We'll rehearse and record there and . . . hey, why don't you come with us? I'll rent you a house on the beach, right in Santa Monica. You can bring the children. You can all be together for a grand vacation, a holiday. What do you say?"

The fear began to leave Angelique's eyes and was replaced by resignation. "Mister Roy, we already live in paradise. Why would we need a vacation? From what?"

She had me. From what, indeed. Why would she want to go into the madness? Into the cutthroat land of show business?

"I really want to do this, Angelique," the Poet said.

"I can see that you do, my love," she said. "It's just that we're so happy here. You are so happy here."

He looked deeply into her eyes. "I am happy, with you. I wouldn't be what I am without you, and my love for you." He smiled at her. "And those children we've created. This is my home, my life. What I do with the band is only for a moment." He laughed, more to himself than to us. "One last youthful indiscretion. A final Dionysian dance. Without the drugs, babes, and booze, of course."

Angelique gave a little laugh. "Well, I should hope so," she said.

"I just want to be supported by the music. Held up, in the air, floating on the ocean of sound. Those icy lines of Roy's. That nightmare-carnival sound, the organ of Dr. Caligari. And the guitar player's liquid bottleneck—like glass it was. And the drummer's power . . . his subtlety. He always listened to my words, and he accented them so perfectly. I loved his drumming. And I miss it, riding on his waves of rhythm while the guitar and organ wove in and out through my ears, howling like banshees. They made me forget everything, except the instant of time between beats. I lived in those milliseconds. There was an eternity there. I felt safe and secure in those instants. Nothing could hurt me in those moments."

"Like the day in the ocean," she said. "When you entered the energy."

"Yes, Angelique. But that day in the ocean was even better than being onstage. That day was the all. Like Rishikesh. And like everyday here with you."

She took his hand and kissed it. "I love you, my darling. You are the sun and the moon to me."

He smiled at her, slowly took his hand from hers and ever so gently stroked her cheek. "No, I am the sun and you are the moon. And Michael and Louise are the stars."

She touched the hand that lay on her cheek, infusing it with her energy. "Then we are the universe, my love."

A silence descended on us. The angel passed over again. Their hands touched, their eyes locked into each other. Their love filled the room, and I was overjoyed for him. He had been through hell and now he was alive. And he was in love.

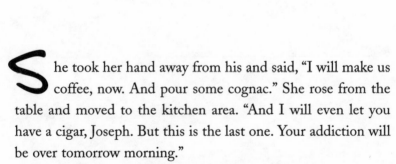

15

She took her hand away from his and said, "I will make us coffee, now. And pour some cognac." She rose from the table and moved to the kitchen area. "And I will even let you have a cigar, Joseph. But this is the last one. Your addiction will be over tomorrow morning."

He smiled at her. "But I'm not addicted."

"Spoken like a true addict," she answered, and set about brewing up our *café filtre*.

"*Touché*," he called to her, and then turned to me. "I'm not. How could I be a cigar junkie? People don't become addicted to cigars."

"Well, from the sound of your cough . . . "

"Alright, alright! I'll stop tomorrow."

"Spoken like a true addict," I said, laughing. He laughed, too, and then coughed again.

"See!" Angelique called out from the stove.

"Stop it, you two," the Poet said.

"We're just tryin' to keep you healthy, don't cha' know," I said with a pronounced drawl.

"And stop mocking my Southern patois, Roy."

"I'll stop tomorrow, I promise."

He couldn't take anymore and punched my arm. "*Momser!*"

"Oww, don't be doin' me like that," I said, rubbing the sore spot. "And what the hell is a momser?"

"It's Yiddish for *wiseguy*. Appropriate, huh? I swear, sometimes I think I never should have listened to you in the first place."

"You mean back on the beach in El Segundo, or today?"

He thought for a second. "Probably both!"

We laughed, easy and secure in each other's company.

And then I whispered to him. "Do you think she's accepted the idea?"

"Honestly, I don't even know if I've accepted the idea."

"But the way you spoke to Angelique, about floating on the music, about really wanting to do it again . . . "

"I'm not sure if that was to convince her, or me."

Now it was my turn to put a hand on his arm. "The people need your words, amigo. They need your hope and your energy."

"I suppose, but it's such a change, Roy. And so much work. I wonder if I'm up to it."

"We'll get you in shape, man. We'll run on the beach, and swim. I can't wait to get in that ocean, and you can teach me some yoga postures. And maybe we'll pump a little iron, too. Hell, if there's not a little gym or something, we can lift rocks. These islands are all granite, anyway."

"Don't make it sound like prison, huh? Lifting rocks?"

"Hey, we'll start easy. Toss a few pebbles into the ocean and gradually work our way up to boulders!"

He shook his head and sighed in mock anguish. "Oh, Lord."

Then Angelique came in to save the moment, carrying a tray of coffee, milk and sugar, brandy, cups and small snifters. "What are you two plotting now?"

"An exercise regimen, Angelique," I said.

"He's going to whup me like a dawg, honey."

"Well, you deserve it," she smiled. "It will be a penance for your past sins. You never did suffer enough."

"I did too," he said. "I suffered. I suffered plenty. In fact, you two are making me suffer right now!"

Angelique and I looked at each other and winked. "It's our job to keep you honest," I said.

"And don't think it's easy, Joseph. You are a very obstinate man."

"I am not," he protested. "I'm just a teddy bear. One of those cute Steiff bears that you like so much."

"You . . . a teddy bear?" I said. "I don't think so."

"Well, I'm *her* teddy bear. I'm not a teddy bear to everyone. Least of all you."

"I should hope not," I said as I punched his arm.

"Oww," he said. "It's not fair your hitting me. You've got Polish piano-player ham fists. I'm just a sensitive and effete poet . . . don't cha' know."

"An out-of-shape poet," said Angelique.

"With a cough," I added.

He sighed. "Can I have some cognac, *s'il vous plait*? This

assault is wearying." He looked at us: first her, then me, then back at her. "You two make a good team . . . of brutalists!"

"Ohh, Joseph. You are my teddy bear. And we won't brutalize you anymore. Will we, mister Roy?"

"Not for tonight, Angelique. But tomorrow I'm going to run him into the ground. Lean like a snake, that's what he's going to be. And rid of that pesky cough. He's going to be like that Muddy Waters album . . . "

"I know it," he said. "*Hard Again.*"

"That's the one, dude."

But Angelique's eyes had gone cold again. She turned her head away as if she had heard something, or seen something she didn't want to allow into the room. She began to pour the coffee and her hand trembled ever so slightly. It was as if something was joining us at the table and only she was aware of it. And it was unwanted.

"I'll get the cigars," the Poet said. "For you, Roy?"

"Sure, I'll have one with you. After all, it's a celebratory cigar. You're alive, we're together, and it's your last one."

He moved to the kitchen and began opening drawers. I looked at Angelique. "Is anything wrong?"

She looked over at me and there were tears in her eyes. "No, nothing is wrong . . . not tonight."

"Angelique," the Poet called, preventing her from saying anything further. "Where is that damned cigar box?"

She wiped her eyes. "In the refrigerator, Joseph." Then she laughed to herself. "I was trying to keep them fresh for you."

He came back to the table with a box of Cohibas. There were four left. He offered me one, took one for himself, and snapped the other two in half.

"That's it," he said. "They're gone. Now, let's have some cognac and enjoy what we have left."

We lit up and the smoke was round and mellow. It went well with the cognac.

"These cigars are like life," he said.

"I hear a silly aphorism coming," I responded.

"Well, this isn't for public consumption. This is just for us. For this moment."

"Okay," I said. "How so?"

He shrugged his shoulders. "Enjoy what's left, right?"

"That's rather simple, isn't it?"

"Yes, but as I sit here with my last cigar . . . I'm going to enjoy what's left."

"Well, I hope there's more left of my life than what's left of this cigar. If that weren't the case then I wouldn't smoke the damn thing at all. Hell, why did I even light it?"

"Roy, you're not getting the point. Life is not as *long* as a cigar, it's *like* a cigar."

"I understand. But why take the chance? I want to live for a long time. Don't you?"

"Of course," he said. He took a deep puff on his cigar, held the globe of it in his mouth, enjoying it, then exhaled a white cloud of smoke. We sat silently, watching it disappear into the ether. He took a sip of his cognac. "Ahh, *la dolce vita,*" he said, contentedly. "Of course I want to live a long time. I didn't when I was young, when I had my whole life in front of me. But now that it's twilight time, I want this sunset to last as long as it can."

He laughed at himself. "Isn't that how it always is? Youth doesn't care. 'Live fast, die young and leave a good looking corpse.' Who's the asshole who said that?"

"I don't know," I said. "But it reminds me of Denny Sullivan. He loved the idea."

"So did I."

"I know, he got it from you!"

"I'll bet it didn't work for him, either."

"No, it didn't. He became a junkie."

"See, it always leads to some kind of addiction."

"It doesn't have to."

"Just because you had self-control, Roy, it doesn't mean that all the rest of us teen rebels did. I had to take it to the limit. I was the Snake Man, hell-bent for leather. The wild child."

"So was Denny. He thought *he* was the wild child. And when you, quote-unquote, died . . . well, he just went over the top. Heroin replaced you in his heart."

"No, not me. His father. See, it's my theory that those downer narcotics fill the hole in your solar plexus that exists because your father simply didn't hug you enough."

"Junkies just need a hug? Come on, that's really simplistic."

"No, Roy. Not simplistic; symbolic."

"How so?"

"The hug is the outward manifestation of your father's protection. Your mother nurtures you and your father protects you; his hug conveys all his wisdom and strength to you by warming your whole chest cavity. He holds your heart to his heart, and you're not afraid. You're protected against the child-fears. You don't know anything of life as a child, and the immensity of it scares the shit out of you. You quake before its awesome power, the sheer weight of it all. It's overwhelming."

"When you're a kid," I added, "Life is beyond all comprehension. You're completely at its mercy."

"Exactly. And that's where your father comes in. He made you, and he protects you. He is your hero. And when he hugs you, he transmits male warmth and power to you, filling that rib cage of yours with security and love."

"But if he doesn't?"

"If he's not there, if he's too busy, if he doesn't have time for you, if he's divorced from your mother, well then that space in your rib harp doesn't get its necessary infusion of warmth. And you grow up with a vacancy there. A void. A hole in your soul."

He took another puff on his cigar and sipped his cognac. "And guess what fills that hole when you're no longer a kid?"

"Heroin?"

"Exactly. It imparts a warmth to the whole body that emanates from the fourth chakra, the heart chakra." And he tapped on his chest with his open palm. "Right here, where the void is. Where daddy's inattention left that great, gaping hole, the heroin now fills you with warmth. You feel good and strong and secure. Maybe for the first time in your life. And, man, of course you want more. Until you're a damned junkie!"

I nodded. "Denny told me about the first time he tried heroin. He said, 'Roy, when I took it, I said to myself . . . this is the way I want to feel for the rest of my life.'"

"For the rest of his life," the Poet repeated. "See, he had found the warmth he was lacking."

"And you knew his father."

"Sure. He was never there for the kid. Divorced from Denny's mother . . . "

"Married about five times, I think."

The Poet laughed. "What was the matter, couldn't he get it right?" And he took Angelique's hand and squeezed it. "It's not very hard. It's just a matter of love, and giving."

Angelique kissed his hand. "You give everything to the other, mister Roy," she said softly. "You give the other your heart."

"And you give the other," the Poet said looking deeply into her eyes, "everything she wants."

"But you must never ask for everything," Angelique said. "Only what is necessary."

"So there's the secret, Roy. Love, and give, and don't ask for it all. Life never intended for us to get it all. You can't have all the things your mind can think of. You can't have a movie star–handsome husband and a career in telecommunications and a perfect little family with two tow-headed kids and a ten-thousand square foot house with five bedrooms, eight baths, a designer kitchen, a cutting garden, a golden Labrador retriever named Spencer, and an SUV and a Mercedes in the garage. You just don't get all that. You can think of it—therefore you want it. But I'm here to tell you," and he went Southern patois again, "y'all ain't gonna get it. Not all that, you ain't."

Then Angelique joined in. "Do I need more than this, mister Roy? Could I be more satisfied? Could I be happier? I love this man, this poet friend of yours. And I love the children we have made together. They are the joy of my life. And when they are grown and have left us, perhaps I will write a book on the care and feeding of a rock star." And she laughed her little bells again.

"A retired rock star, my dear," he said.

"No," I said. "The very complex story of a rock star who was dead, but not really dead, just retired, who then comes out of retirement for one last incredible round of art, poetry and music, and a journey into the one."

Angelique smiled, "Perhaps that's one for you to write. I would be more concerned with the day-to-day life of that retired rock star. And how to deal with the arrogance."

"What?!" the Poet exclaimed. "What arrogance?"

"You don't even know, do you, Joseph?"

"Well, perhaps I do have a bit of an inflated view of myself. But I wouldn't call it arrogance . . . Would you?"

"Yes, Joseph," she said.

I had to laugh. She had pinned him, just as he had pinned every-one back in the days of his stardom. He was adroit at pointing out people's flaws, and now she was in his life to do the same to him.

The Poet lowered his head. "Guilty as charged." Then he looked up at me, "What can I say, man? She always has my best interests at heart. When it comes to me, I know she's right."

"Then you're very lucky, my friend."

"I was right when I told you to go to India those many years ago, wasn't I?" Angelique said softly.

"You certainly were, darling." The Poet took another puff on his cigar and sipped his cognac.

I stared at him. "Angelique told you to go to India?"

"That's right. She was the girl on the beach. Remember?"

"The teenager. The café-au-lait girl in the cutoffs and the bikini top. That was Angelique?!"

"Yes, this woman who just cooked you dinner is the same girl who knew I could find the answers in India."

"My god, no wonder you're with her. The two of you are your own magic circle."

"Just like the band, amigo."

"Angelique, how did you know to tell him to go to India? You were just a child."

"But we grow up very quickly in the tropics," she said. "And I had read a book about the Buddha. He was a wonderful man, a good man. And I knew—call it that feminine intuition that you men are always speaking of—that Joseph wanted to become a good man. And even though we are all Christians here, India is not so far away. We know the yogis are there, and that the Buddha was there. So I told him to go. Even though I loved him from the moment I saw him that day on the beach, I told him to go to India."

"Knowing you might never see him again?"

"Yes, but hoping somehow he would come back to me. I knew I couldn't have him then. He was not complete, yet."

"And after all you had been through," I said to the Poet, "you still came back to her."

"Well, I came back to the Seychelles. But I must admit, even in India, the image of Angelique entered my dreams. I didn't come back here looking for her, but she was like the scent of a perfume that lingers somewhere in your memory. I couldn't get her out of my unconscious mind. She didn't occupy my waking thoughts, but I told myself that if I ever did see her again I would thank her profusely for saying to me . . . "

"I think you should go to India, mister," Angelique said, completing his thought for him and reenacting the moment. She brought the Poet's hand to her lips and kissed it. "You occupied my *waking* mind almost every day. I loved you and I prayed for a day when I would see you again. And St. Rita answered my prayers."

"St. Rita? Why did you pray to her?" I asked.

"She is the patron saint of the impossible, mister Roy."

"Well, she's certainly taking care of *this* household," I said. "Look at the three of us. What are the odds of us all being here together? Pretty impossible, I'd say."

"Then here's to St. Rita," the Poet said, raising his glass for a toast. We joined him and sipped our cognac in honor of that saint from Cascia, Italy.

"Of course I don't believe in any of it," the Poet said.

"Oh, Joseph. You are such a cynic."

"No, darling. A skeptic. But I do believe in the holographic universe and our ability to influence it through our thoughts."

"And through our prayers," said Angelique.

He smiled at her. "Your prayers *are* your thoughts, Angelique."

"How did you two find each other again?" I asked.

"Very simple. After coming back from India, I found a room for myself in a little pension. Then I thought I ought to get some gainful employment. At first I thought something physical, something I could do with my hands. I had never done manual labor before and I thought it would be good for me. So I got a job, believe it or not, with the fishermen. We'd go out every day on the boats, cast nets, and haul them in. Tough work, hauling those nets. Rubbed my hands raw, man. And the rowing! Jesus, what hard work. But I stayed with it and got calluses the size of quarters. My one failing was I didn't have a knack with the fish. They wouldn't jump into my net. And the old men said to me that I wasn't intended to be a fisherman. They said the fish only respond to men who love them. They said the fish are willing to sacrifice themselves to our love and understanding of them. And I must admit, I was indifferent to the fish. I didn't love them. I certainly didn't understand them."

"It would be rather difficult to actually understand a fish," I joked.

"Not for the real fisherman. They're into those fish like the American Indians were into the buffalo. There's a symbiotic relationship there. And I wasn't part of it. I suppose I could have become part of it, in twenty years or so. Sort of like a Zen master painting a *sumi-e* circle. Nothing to it, but it takes a lifetime to perfect. I didn't think I wanted to spend twenty years trying to relate to fish."

Angelique smiled. "Even St. Rita would have had trouble with that task, my love."

He laughed. "Indeed."

"So, what happened? How did you two meet again?"

"Well, one of the old men said to me, 'Joseph, forget about fishing. You are a storyteller!' See, I used to entertain the men with tales of American rock and roll. Stories of us on the road, in the recording studio, and all manner of debauchery. Being men of the sea they of course loved the tales of debauchery best. 'Just go and write your stories,' the old man said."

"And did you?" I asked, hoping he had.

"Hell no. Relive that madness? No way. It's one thing to spin some yarns for a bunch of lusty fishermen, but I wasn't about to sit in my room, all alone, and allow those demons back into my life."

"What did you do?"

"The newspaper. I would write about life today for the little local newspaper. That is if they would have me. And luckily they needed someone to fill in a slot that had just been vacated. And this is the best part of the story. Guess who was a copy girl at the newspaper?"

"I don't believe it . . . "

"Bingo! St. Rita in action," the Poet exclaimed.

"My prayers had been answered," Angelique said. "I saw him and I saw my entire life unfold before me. I saw our love, this house, the children. I saw him writing his poems. I saw him in my arms and I could feel him inside of me. I saw everything that day he walked into the newspaper's office."

"Sometimes I think she's like a witch, or something," the Poet said.

Angelique smiled. "A good witch, I should hope, Joseph."

"You're the voodoo queen of New Orleans. A very good witch, Angelique."

"And you saw all of this?" I asked.

"Everything, mister Roy. It just flashed before my eyes. It was like a dream in which you see a future event before it happens in everyday reality." She paused, remembering, and then continued. "He did not even recognize me when he came into the office that day, seeking a job."

"Darling, how could I? You had become a woman. When I left for India you were a girl. Of course a beautiful girl."

"With some degree of wisdom, too," I added.

"Indeed, Roy. Wisdom . . . or witchy powers."

"It's just a little gift of sight, mister Roy," Angelique protested. "It's not witchy, Joseph. And you know it."

"I know. But sometimes I can't resist teasing you."

"Is that why your son said that he knew I was coming, Angelique?" I asked. "You saw me arriving and told Michael?"

"Yes," she said. I knew you were coming."

"She told me to go to the Bar Gauguin," the Poet said. "She said she had a feeling something would happen, something important for me. I pay attention to her feelings. But I had no idea she had arranged this whole thing!"

"Including sending me those poems."

She looked at the Poet, sheepishly. "I took some pages from your notebooks, Joseph."

The Poet smiled. "Very clever."

"What about the newspaper, Angelique? Did you arrange that, too?"

"Hardly, mister Roy. I didn't even know he was back from India. St. Rita arranged it."

"But I recognized her soon enough. I think the very next day. I asked her to dinner that night, didn't I, Angelique?"

"Yes, you did. I was so delighted to see you again. I wanted to know everything that had happened to you."

"And I told her. It was so good to share my journey with someone. Especially the girl . . . "

Angelique protested, "The woman."

"Yes, now the woman who had set me on the trail. It was such a pleasure to actually share my life story with someone. I had never done that before. I opened myself up to another human being."

"And a beautiful one," I said.

"More importantly, an intelligent one, and a receptive one," the Poet said. "She understood everything I was saying."

"How long did it take you to fall in love with her, my friend?"

The Poet laughed. "Oh, a long time. About a week."

Angelique smiled. "It was much longer for me. It took me about a day."

They both laughed. And they were so good together that I was elated for him. He had found what he was looking for. He had found himself and he had found his woman. They were complete, and they were living together in paradise. At one and at peace with each other.

"He asked me to marry him within three months of our first date," Angelique said.

"I was bursting for her," the Poet said. "She had to be my wife. I could share everything with her, and she made me crazy in the head. I was in a kind of crazy love-hell. I still am, but those were the first runaway throes of passion. I wanted her like I had never wanted anything before, including our music. I was in a fire. My heart was detonating, my loins were roaring, my mind was in a delirium . . . " He paused to catch his breath. It was as if he was reliving those first days and was lost in the memory.

"You make me blush," Angelique said. "I didn't know I had that kind of effect on you."

"Oh, you did, my love." He took her hand. "And you still do. I just try to keep it under control now."

Angelique squeezed his hand. "I love you, Joseph."

"I love you, too, my Angelique."

I could only sit there in silence, looking at my friend and his beautiful wife dissolving into one another's eyes. They were in their own world, and they needed nothing else. He was home. And alive.

The Poet turned to me and took my hand. "I'm so very happy today, Roy. I am a completely fulfilled man. My wife, my children, and you, my old and dear friend. I have everything. Everything I could ever ask for, or need, or want. It's all right here, right now."

Then he sighed. A great, free and luxurious sigh. The sigh of a man at peace.

"I'm tired, now. This has been quite a day for me. If you don't mind, Angelique will see you back to your hotel. Is that alright with you, darling?"

"Of course it is, Joseph. You rest now. I'm glad your surprise was so much fun for you. I'd hoped it would be."

"You always know how to please me, my love," he said as he rose from the table and kissed her softly on the lips. "I love you," he whispered, and then turned to me. "Roy . . . I kind of love you, too. You big organ of death, Slavic iceman, blurt it out know it all." He slapped me on the back, laughed, and was gone.

Through the closed door of the bedroom I heard him cough again. Angelique and I could only sit there, quietly listening to that sound. Then she looked at me and spoke softly.

"Come, mister Roy. I will take you back to Victoria. There is something I have to tell you. Something you are not going to want to hear."

16

The jungle had descended even further into deep blackness. Angelique held a flashlight to illuminate the path. She had brought with her a canvas tote bag that she had flung over her shoulder. It seemed rather heavy for a walk back to town. I was curious as to its contents, but of course I was most curious, and fearful, about what Angelique was going to say to me.

We walked in silence as she collected herself. "I sent you the poems, mister Roy. I wanted you to come to him so he could tell you his story. So the two of you could see each other again. The only thing he regrets about his hoax is that he had to fool you, too, and the other people close to him. I knew he wanted to unburden himself to you, but he didn't know how."

"He could have just called me," I said." "He could have written me."

"Well, that's not his way. Too direct. If he had called you, it would have lacked that sense of mystery that he loves. You know how he loves drama."

"Yes, Angelique. Everything with him was a drama. We could never do anything simply in our band days. We could never go from one day to the next without some sort of crisis being created by your husband."

"He has not changed that much. Except for the crisis, we don't have any of that. But the drama is still with us. And I love it. We are never bored."

"He was always a challenge to live with," I said.

"No, not anymore. He is just, how to say it, theatrical. He is always writing something grand in his mind. We live in a movie and every incident carries a profound meaning with it."

"The drama of existence, don't cha' know," I said in his Southern drawl. She smiled.

"Well, a direct phone call or letter would have lacked that drama," she said. "So I hit upon the idea of sending you little pieces of his poetry, from his journals."

"That's why it was his handwriting . . . but my name was typed. You just typed 'J' and 'Gauguin' on a page of his journal."

"Yes, just a few words to whet your appetite. I hoped that would make it more interesting for you. Sort of a mystery."

"It worked."

"I'm glad. Because for all I knew, you could have been completely removed from the past. Indifferent."

"Never, Angelique. I love him. I always did."

'I know that now, mister Roy. But if you actually came with so little that I sent you, if you even, for a moment, believed it was him, then I knew everything would be as I hoped it would."

I put my arm around her shoulder and hugged her to me. "And it is as you hoped, Angelique. Why, we're even going to put the band back together. We're going to create music and he's going to sing again."

"That's something I never thought would happen. I wanted you to come and I wanted him to see you, to tell you his life. To let you know that he didn't die in Paris, and what an adventure he went on, and to see what a good man he has become. And I wanted him to be at peace concerning you. But I never imagined that the two of you would think to reunite your band again. That thought never occurred to me."

"Well, you don't think like a musician, Angelique. You're not a performer. But he is, and so am I. The people are going to love his message . . . his poetry. The music is going to be great and he's going to be in the spotlight again. Reborn!"

"No, I'm sorry," she said with a great firmness in her voice. "You can't take him away."

"But you can come with us. You can bring the children. We can get them into the Crossroads School in Santa Monica. It's very good. Or we'll hire a private tutor, or they can just run on the beach and experience a new city, a new way of life. Six months of goofing off—of course we'll make them read lots of books. It would be good for them."

"Six months, mister Roy?"

"Yes, that's all the time we'll need to rehearse and record. The drummer and the guitar player will be out of their minds, ecstatic, when they hear the news that he's alive. They'll be so excited to get back to work that ideas will just come bursting out of them. We'll *all* be charged with energy. Filled with light from your husband's words, and boiling over with creativity."

I took her hand and looked deeply into her eyes. "Six months, Angelique. Six months is all we'll need."

She squeezed my hand, then turned away, unable to look at me. She stared at the great canopy of stars and a deep sigh escaped from her, a sigh that seemed to come from some hidden place in her soul.

"He only has about that long to live," she said to the heavens. "He is dying."

I stopped cold. "What are you talking about? He can't be dying!"

Her eyes came out of the sky into mine. They were large with anguish. "I'm sorry, mister Roy. It is true. He has cancer of the lungs. And it has spread into his lymph nodes. There is nothing they can do. The cancer has gone too far. It has metastasized."

"This can't be true. Please, tell me this a joke, one of his jokes."

"He is dying," she said.

My mind raced for answers, for a way to reverse this terrible news. "Then we'll take him to the States to treat him. Surely it can be stopped. We have the best doctors, the newest techniques. They can cure him."

"I don't think so," she said softly, resigned to the Fates. "He will be dead in six months."

"But Denny Sullivan had lung cancer. He smoked cigarettes for years. Radiation and chemotherapy cured him! We can cure your husband, too! Denny has a brother John, in Beverly Hills, a great doctor. He'll know what to do . . . who to see."

"Did the cancer metastasize in your Denny? Had it spread to his lymph nodes?"

I felt a sickness in my stomach. "No, it hadn't."

"That's why they could save him. It was still in his lungs. With Joseph, the cancer has gone wild in him." She sighed again. "Nothing can stop it." Then she buried her face in her hands. "He will die, my Joseph will die." She began to sob. Her body jerked with spasms of anguish and unbearable sorrow. "Oh, mister Roy. I love him so much."

I put my arms around her and held her close to me, trying to comfort her. And I thought of the Fates—the three sisters— they had spun his thread, woven his life, and would now cut the thread. The fabric was complete. His life story was finished. His exile was truly over. And I was devastated.

We stood like that for I don't know how long. And then Angelique's sobs subsided and she was able to speak. "But at least we had him, didn't we? He came back from India for me."

"And he has been reborn for me, Angelique."

"Then that is all we can ask for," she said. "Destiny had a great and full life planned for him. And we were able to share it with him. How lucky we are."

She sighed again, wiped her tears, and took my hand. "Come, I will take you back."

And we moved off, into that mysterious black, under a dome of radiant stars. We walked in silence, and I knew that she had the right perspective. How lucky we were to have known him, to have loved him.

Finally, I spoke. "He doesn't know, then."

"No. I found out two days ago. I saw no reason to tell him. I will, soon. After you are gone."

"But he must know something. He went in for tests, didn't he?"

"A routine checkup. He said now that he was no longer a pup, perhaps he should have a full physical exam."

I nodded. "Just to find out how the machine is running."

"His is running out. And I knew it. That's why I sent you the poems. I knew something was wrong. I could feel it, but I had no idea how ill he was. When he said it was time for a checkup, I agreed and I hoped my feelings would be proven wrong. But they weren't. I swear, sometimes I hate this power . . . this clairvoyance. Sometimes I wish I didn't have it at all."

"But I'm here because of that second sight of yours. And he is a happy man tonight. He told me everything."

She smiled. "Then he is unburdened."

"Yes. And you saw the smile on his face at supper. He was with his wife, his children, and his friend. He was a man at peace with himself and his world. But he won't be happy when he finds me gone and you tell him of the inevitable."

"The death part won't bother him. He knows where he's going. But not making music with you, that will be hard for him."

"Actually, Angelique, it wasn't his idea. I talked him into it. I hadn't met you or the children. I had no idea what his life here had become, and all I could think of was what we once had and how we could do it again. I'm the one who wanted it. He was reluctant, but he finally gave in. I think the idea of getting his new perspective out to the world was what intrigued him."

"Didn't he seem excited about singing again?" she asked.

"Not particularly."

"He loves to sing around the house."

"From sheer joy. He's like a songbird with you, just singing for the love of life."

"He is a happy man, mister Roy."

"I could see that when we were all together. And I must confess, the thought occurred to me that perhaps it was wrong to take him away from this, his real love. But his story, his words . . ."

"They should be heard," she finished for me. "People should know of his journey, and his discovery of his true self."

"Exactly, Angelique. And they should know of the possibilities for themselves."

Then she removed the canvas tote bag from her shoulder. "That is why I brought this, mister Roy." She handed it to me. "In here are his journals and his poems. Take them back to America. Do with them what you will. If you publish anything, or make any songs, set up a trust fund for our children's college education. I want them to go to school."

I held the tote bag to my chest. "I will take care of your children, and I will take care of you, Angelique. Just tell me if you need anything. Anything at all for your family. For him."

And then we left the dark vegetation behind and approached the outskirts of the town.

"I will write you if I need something, mister Roy. But I think we will be all right. That is, until he makes the leap upward. Then it will be hard . . . without him."

I put my arm around her again. "If you wish, come to visit California, Angelique. Our home is open to you—you and the children. It would be a great adventure for all of you. I'll show you everything."

"But that is where he was. Everything would remind me of him." She took my hand and we slowly continued our walk into Victoria. "Thank you, but I think we will stay here. This is our home."

We walked in silence as all around us the town began to turn off its lights, buttoning up for the night. "There's my hotel, Angelique," I said as we neared the Pension Nicole. "I can make it from here."

She wrapped her arms around me and held me tightly. "I'm so glad you came. It was important for him."

I kissed her softly on the cheek. "I'm going to leave in the morning, Angelique. As soon as I can. I don't want to say goodbye to him, ever—this will be our goodbye. And tell him I love him."

She took her arms from around me and put one hand on my cheek. She looked into my eyes and then kissed me lightly on the lips. It was the taste of a tropical·flower.

"Goodbye, mister Roy. I will tell him, and I will write to you." She handed me a folded piece of paper. "Here, he wrote this yesterday. His last poem."

And she turned and headed off, back into the jungle, back toward her home . . . and the Poet. I stood there and watched her. Before she disappeared into the vegetation she turned and called to me. "Mister Roy. Walk in the light."

I moved to a street lamp and opened the piece of paper, his last poem, and read it through my tears.

> *Give me songs*
> *to sing.*
> *And emerald dreams*
> *to dream.*
> *I'll give you love,*
> *unfolding.*
>
> *Sun!*

THE END